About the Author

Frank Dirscherl (b. 1973) is the Amazon bestselling author of *The Wraith* and editor of *Beyond the Lens*. His series of *The Wraith Adventures* books have been enjoyed by multitudes of readers the world over. Other books in the series include *Valley of Evil*, *Crossfire*, *Cult of the Damned* and *Cry of the Werewolf*, with more to come.

A professionally certified library technician, who has been working in libraries for more than twenty years, Dirscherl has also worked at a medical practice in a data entry position, covered books for a book wholesale company, and as a lecturer to children on the merits, and writing, of comic books.

He lives on the south coast of New South Wales, Australia, with his beautiful wife Jennifer, where he is currently working on his latest piece of fiction.

For more information on Frank, please visit his website at
www.frankdirscherl.com

Praise for *The Wraith*
Amazon bestseller

"I love the coloring job and specially the 'glowing' eyes on the chest of the character."
– Guillermo del Toro, director, *Blade II, Hellboy I & II*

"I liked the story a lot... It's a very strong debut."
Steve Englehart, writer, *Detective Comics, The Avengers, Green Lantern*

"I have read the novel (I couldn't put it down)... It is amazing to see how her (Leena) character evolves from Part I to Part II. At first she appears as every other 'girlfriend' in an action film, but those twelve months that pass obviously change her as a person and I love the person she becomes: tougher, but still human."
– Amber Moelter, actress, *Catwoman: Copycat*

"I finished *The Wraith* book last night. I must say I enjoyed it quite a bit. The scenes kept playing in my head like a big budget Hollywood film. I mentioned earlier that I enjoy when the hero is put to the test physically and doesn't win the battle unscathed. Boy, (Frank) delivered that in spades!"
– Jeff Welborn, artist, *Nightmare World, The Wraith*

"Genius + sweat + dedication = hard hittin' hero action! Go Aussie!"
– Dan Lennard, writer, *People* magazine

Praise for *Valley of Evil*

"The second Wraith novel is an improvement, I think. Right from the start Dirscherl throws you into the middle of crazy action.... This book is a whole lot of superheroic pulp fun, and the good news is there seems to be more to come...I look forward to some more of the same."

      – Richard Scott, *Super Reader* website

"I think (Dirscherl) really captured a noir element with (his) voice."

      – Joshua Gamon, writer, *Abigail & Rox, Digital Webbing Presents*

"I did quite enjoy the books. Best of all, it wasn't overly sex-filled or gory—I can't stand most modern superhero comics that show such things or have the heroes just swear and swear. So *The Wraith* (and *Valley of Evil*) was just up my alley."

      – Greg Gick, writer, *The Werewolf of Rutherford Grange, Tales of the Shadowmen, Secret Agent X Vol. 2*

"The Dread Avenger is back. After battling the Cobra in his first prose adventure, The Wraith returns to face all new challenges from Metro City's greatest villains, most notably Hong Kong drug kingpin Ma Tzi. As with his first Wraith novel, Frank Dirscherl treats us to a pulp-inspired adventure that keeps readers on the edge of their seat. You have to read this novel in one sitting."

      – Bobby Nash, writer, *Evil Ways, Fantastix, Lance Star*

"In the past five years there has been a tremendous resurgence in pulp fiction centering on the old heroic pulps. Young writers have started taking up the mantle of old masters like Walter Gibson and Lester Dent and begun creating their own avengers in tales of genuine purple prose. Among the best of this new generation of wordsmiths is Australian, Frank Dirscherl and the exploits of his modern pulp paladin, The Wraith. This is grand pulp!"

   – Ron Fortier, writer, *The Spider, Brother Bones, Domino Lady*

Praise for *Crossfire*

"Stephen did a fantastic job of bringing Frank Dirscherl's character to life!"
- Adam DiTroia, composer, *The Wraith: Eyes of Judgment*, MTV, Fox Sports

"Loved the book!! Can't wait for the next installment..."
- Larry Mainland, actor, *The Walking Dead, Lawless, The Three Stooges*

"The action comes swift, and doesn't stop until the final pages. *Crossfire* tells a great story of betrayal and revenge."
- C.R. Blevins, writer, *A Western Tale*

Praise for *Cult of the Damned*

"Only by the first three pages, Frank Dirscherl wonderfully captures a dark and mysterious atmosphere, one that leaves the reader with a cryptic and eerie sensation; one that makes me cold just thinking about it."

> – Rennie Cowan, writer/director, *The Thriller Idol: A Tribute to the Legacy of Michael Jackson, Kade the Conqueror*

"Frank Dirscherl pulls you into the world of The Wraith from the first sentence and refuses to let you go until the last one."

> – Stephen J. Semones, writer/director, *Beyond the Lens, Crossfire, The Wraith: Eyes of Judgment*

"The Wraith is one of my favorite characters and every time Frank Dirscherl puts pen to paper I know I'm in for a real treat."

> – A.P. Fuchs, writer, *The Axiom-man Saga, The Way of the Fog, Undead World trilogy*

By Frank Dirscherl

Fiction

Titles in *The Wraith Adventures* series
(in story order)
The Wraith
Valley Of Evil
Crossfire (edited)
Cult of the Damned
Cry of the Werewolf
Werewolves Attack! in *Metahumans vs Werewolves* (short story)
Zombies Attack! in *Metahumans vs the Undead* (short story)

Attack of the Birdman in *Lance Star – Sky Ranger Vol. 1* (short story)

Non-Fiction

*The Wraith: Eyes of Judgment – The Official Script Book
& Movie Guide* (with Stephen Semones)
Waterfall After Dark in *The Hitchers of Oz* (short story)
Beyond the Lens (edited)

Comic Books

The Wraith #0
The Wraith: The Collected Editions #1-3
Curse of the Cortes Stone (with Joe Martino & Scott Story)

www.trinitycomics.com

VALLEY OF EVIL

The Wraith Adventures #2

by

Frank Dirscherl

TRINITY COMICS
WOLLONGONG

TRINITY COMICS
PO Box 31
Wollongong NSW 2520

ISBN 978-0-646-90809-0

PUBLISHED BY TRINITY COMICS, August 2013
www.trinitycomics.com
FRONT COVER PENCILS by Al Rio
FRONT COVER INKS by Jeff Austin
FRONT COVER COLORS by Splash!
COVER LAYOUT AND DESIGN AND INTERIOR DESIGN by Frank Dirscherl
FIRST PUBLISHED (TWICE) IN 2006
THIRD EDITION

For more on *Valley of Evil*
visit www.trinitycomics.com

Text set in Garamond. Printed and bound in the USA

National Library of Australia Cataloguing-in-Publication entry

Author: Dirscherl, Frank, 1973- author.

Title: Valley of evil / Frank Dirscherl.

Edition: Third Edition

ISBN: 9780646908090 (paperback)

Series: Wraith adventures ; 2.

Subjects: The Wraith (Fictitious character)
Superheroes.

Dewey Number: A823.4

For my wife Jennifer; and to Nat...thanks for being the 'villain'

VALLEY OF EVIL

~ Chapter 1 ~

The expansive grounds of the estate of Metro City's latest player in crime, Ma Tzi, were patrolled by several burly, armed guards. All appeared well equipped and to be the kind to shoot first and ask questions later. As they patrolled, they gripped their weapons tightly, straining to see in the darkness of the warm, late spring night.

Crouched in a nearby grove of shrubbery, The Wraith and his assistant, Max Horton, watched on intently, waiting for their opportunity to move. Max glanced over to The Wraith for any sign, but there was none. The Wraith remained crouched, his eyes squinting with concentration through narrow slits, his muscles flexed and ready for action—a jungle predator stalking its prey.

As the patrols moved away from their vantage point, a thin, tight smile appeared on The Wraith's lips. He motioned to Max, and they made their move, leaving the safety of their darkened hideaway. The two sped forth, sprinting effortlessly for a medium-sized bungalow alongside the estate's Olympic-sized swimming pool. Ma Tzi, the self-proclaimed Dragon of his empire—a drug lord—had made Metro City his home in the months since the city's partial destruction at the hands of the Cobra. Resident crime lord Robert Latham's empire had taken a strong hit then, and Tzi, the Hong Kong expatriate who already had control of the drug trade of several cities on the West Coast of the US, had seen his opportunity to take control from a rival he no doubt perceived to be weak and vulnerable.

What he found, however, was far from that. True, Latham's empire had suffered somewhat during the Cobra's offensive against the city, but Latham could hardly be described as weak. Metro City had been wracked with an intense urban war between the two crime factions. For months, attacks both subtle and overt had been made by both sides, with neither gaining any real advantage. The Wraith had watched on, unable to intervene due to the serious injuries he sustained in defeating the Cobra and his army of the homeless, but now that he had healed, he had to take action, lest his city fall waste to the war now being waged.

The Wraith and Max reached the front of the bungalow quickly and hunched down tight against the front wall. Their actions remained undetected, and they were alone in the black shadows of the night. Max removed from his back a small backpack and pulled from it night-vision goggles and a small lock-pick.

"With the alarm already disabled," Max whispered, "this'll be a cinch. In-and-out." He put on the goggles.

"Open the door, quickly," The Wraith whispered tersely.

Max had the door open in an instant, and the duo crept inside the darkened abode. The Wraith pressed against his cowl at his right temple and special night-vision lenses dropped into place over his eyes. Max was The Wraith's chief assistant in his war on crime, and also his mechanic, chauffeur and inventor of all the gadgets he used in his struggle against evil. These special lenses were but a small fraction of the equipment at The Wraith's disposal.

The interior of the bungalow appeared as expected. It was one large open-plan room filled with pool and garden equipment. Max shuffled forward through the room then turned to face The Wraith.

"Chief, you sure your intel was on the money?" Max asked softly.

The Wraith silently walked past him and moved along a side window. Ignoring Max, he ran his fingers under the window ledge until he reached a spot at the bottom left-hand corner. A section of the floor adjacent to the window slid open, revealing a narrow staircase burrowing down into a black abyss.

"I'm sure," The Wraith said.

Max joined The Wraith in standing before the staircase. With their night-vision lenses in place, they could see the stairs journey down into the unknown, though in this case, they knew exactly where it led.

"You sure you don't want me down there with you?" Max asked.

"I need you to stay here and stand point. Tzi's men could come along this way at any moment, and I need you here to distract them long enough for me to get the job done and for us to escape."

Max looked at The Wraith with concerned eyes, but said nothing. The Wraith knew Max well enough to know that despite his assistant's concerns, Max would follow him at his word, every time.

The Wraith dropped into the darkness, leaving Max to stand guard. The Wraith had received a tip-off from his contact within Tzi's camp that, unlike most crime lords, Tzi kept most of his operations close to home. In this case, his major drug distillation plant was located right under his own estate, in a secret and well-secured underground den. The audacity of the drug lord didn't fail to gall the Dread Avenger of the Underworld.

A few seconds passed before The Wraith reached the bottom of the stairs, where he was met by a large, and obviously sturdy, door. To the left of the door about chest high was an intricate security keypad. The Wraith's contact had given him the access code. He keyed it in. Success.

The door slid open with a whoosh of gears as the lights strobed on automatically. The Wraith quickly retracted his night-vision lenses and took in the incredible sight before him. It was as though he were standing on the floor of an enormous warehouse. Canisters were carefully stacked four-high in innumerable rows on either side, stretching all the way to the far wall. In the center was Tzi's laboratory equipment, no doubt for discovering new, more addictive drugs to flood the city—indeed the country—with. The Wraith clenched his jaw. Tzi hadn't wasted any time in the months since he invaded Metro City; The Wraith partially blamed himself for the apparent ease at which Tzi had made the city his home. He had been badly wounded in his battle with the Cobra, and had required months of recuperation and rehabilitation. Even now, though stronger and well-healed, he still felt twinges of pain every now and then, and he damned the fates that had brought this new evil to his city.

He focused on the task at hand. From his belt he removed several small explosive nodes and scanned the warehouse for strategic points to plant them. Moving deftly amongst the evidence of Tzi's evil, The Wraith hastily secured the nodules in various places throughout the entirety of the warehouse.

The Wraith retreated swiftly, and made sure to close the warehouse door behind him, securing it in place. He leaped up the stairs three at a time, and soon returned to Max, still stationed as he was by the door of the bungalow.

"Everything's in place. The explosives are set on a ten-minute fuse. Get ready to get out of here," The Wraith whispered.

As they began to open the door, a multitude of small arms fire reverberated across the grounds of the estate. Max shut the door tight and looked at him. He motioned Max to remain quiet and took his place by the door. He opened the door ever so slightly, just enough to peek out into the night. What he saw was nothing short of full-blown warfare—Tzi's men raced around in panic, firing wildly in all directions. Something or someone had caused them to react like this and The Wraith knew it could only be Robert Latham, launching yet another offensive against his arch rival. His mind buzzed with a strategy to not only escape their current position—for it was potentially about to disintegrate in an explosion of intense fury—but to take advantage of the disarray caused by Latham's attack.

The Wraith smiled.

"You've got something planned, I can see it," Max said as the sounds of battle raged ever stronger.

"This is going to be a night both Latham and Tzi will never forget."

They waited for their chance, then, when the raging battle outside seemed to have moved away from them, they quickly slipped out into the night.

* * * * * *

Inside his massive mansion stronghold, Ma Tzi was anxious. He was the average height of a Chinese male, with very short black hair, and such smooth skin as to almost defy his middle age. Tzi sat in a large room filled with monitors where he ordinarily saw almost every corner of his estate. Several, however, were blacked out. Tzi remained seated while his men worked frantically, trying to re-establish the connections.

"Hurry!" the crime lord yelled, his English carrying only a hint of a Chinese accent. "I must know what is happening. I must be able to co-ordinate my defenses."

"Power to sections seven and eight have been cut. We haven't been able to restore them yet," replied one eager young employee.

Tzi stood. He felt the veins in his temples throbbing with fury. "Damn you, Mr. Latham! Why won't you sit down and accept the inevitable?" he asked, more of himself than to his staff. "Why won't you accept my gracious offer and join me? Surely you must realize this action is fruitless? Surely you must realize the only way you can survive in this city is to work for me!"

Tzi walked over to the communications hub of his surveillance center and barked orders to his men outside, who battled to stave off the invasion by Latham's forces.

"Push them back, my warriors," Tzi commanded in his smooth, cultured yet deep voice. "This is but another of Mr.

Latham's 'exploratory actions.' Deal with them as you have in the past!"

Tzi turned and faced his surveillance crew. He smiled and returned to his seat.

"Now, please restore the power to sections seven and eight as quickly as possible. I do not wish to be caught off guard again."

* * * * * *

The Wraith had ordered Max to safety, then continued through the Tzi estate. Now with this conflagration having started, The Wraith thought one man could squeeze through the intense defenses where two could not, and above all, he had a much more important job for Max to accomplish, one which only Max and Leena could do while he remained here in this stronghold of evil. He listened, and knew the site of the battle had shifted to the northern-most extent of Tzi's estate. Latham's forces were being pushed back, as they had been in their previous attempts. Still, The Wraith thought, this kind of work was better done alone. He crept toward the main mansion. Flattening himself against the wall of the superb Mandarin-designed structure, he inched toward the corner, and carefully peered around. Spying the front door, he saw it well-guarded by at least four armed men. The Wraith pulled back and thought for a moment. Entering the house, even one as well protected as this one, was relatively easy for him, but sneaking inside undetected was, this time, not his intended purpose. He wanted in, and to make an impact in doing so. So, that left the front entrance which, despite the danger, suited him perfectly.

The four guards watched and waited for any signs of movement. They were prepared, it seemed, for any eventuality, and would rebuke any invasion with brute force. *But they're not prepared for me*, The Wraith thought. They remained still, appearing to be following the sounds of gunfire moving away. One turned to face the other and in doing so saw what the others did not.

The Wraith dropped behind them, raising his cloak.

"Holy!" the guard cried out, raising his weapon, ready to fire at the Dread Avenger.

The Wraith grabbed the smallest of the four hapless guards from behind and tossed him at the guard who was about to shoot. With both of them temporarily out of action, The Wraith settled his attention toward the other two.

One of the remaining guards was able to raise his weapon toward him, but The Wraith caught the gun and pushed it skyward. The gun went off. The Wraith delivered a powerful blow to the guard's stomach, sending him to his knees. The other guard swung at him with his weapon, but The Wraith rolled swiftly to one side, only catching a glimpse as the swinging weapon smacked into the other guard—who was on his knees—knocking him out. On his feet in an instant, The Wraith executed a leg-sweep, sending the standing guard to the ground hard. A karate chop ended the battle. The Wraith turned and glared at the first two guards lying close to him. They were awake and had watched the fight with fear in their eyes. Their weapons were lost.

"Leave—NOW!" The Wraith ordered as the Eyes of Judgment on his chest began to crackle with energy, gleaming a sickening yellow. Fearful for their lives, the two guards stood—and ran!

The Wraith spun on his heels and made his way to the front door. He had a message for Tzi this night, and nothing would prevent him from delivering it. As he reached the porch, two more guards streamed forth from the house. The

Wraith dealt each of them powerful blows to the face without breaking stride, rendering them unconscious. He entered the Tzi mansion and saw the ornate Chinese décor throughout. Knowing the floor plan of the house to perfection—*Know thy enemy*, thought The Wraith—he marched through the maze of rooms, encountering more guards along the way. He made quick work of all of them.

* * * * * *

Inside his surveillance center, the Dragon looked on with concern. He had been happy as he watched Latham's men fall back, happy as his warriors—as he so described them—had once again repelled the horde of his enemy. Now, however, he had heard the shots from close by and knew that something was amiss. The cameras had failed to pick anything up except shadows...and that worried him. Normally a cool and calm man, with an almost kindly disposition, Tzi nevertheless realized the potential damage Latham, or others, could do while he was not in total control of his surroundings, which he always had been when seated here. His men milled about, continuing to frantically work to bring the power back up to various parts of the estate, but it was slow going. Latham's forces had done a stellar job, and only so much could be done in this central control base before other repair work had to be done elsewhere. Tzi sat motionless, his mind reeling, thinking of a way to make Latham pay dearly for this transgression.

In an instant, the relative calm of the room was shattered by an explosion which blew the room's double-door completely off, careening it forward. It slammed into some of the intricate computer equipment. A pall of smoke erupted from the shattered doorway. The room's occupants had been thrown back against the far wall behind Tzi, who remained in his seat. For interminable seconds, silence reigned. Then, emerging from the smoke, appearing briefly as though some creature from hell appeared two shimmering, eerie lights instantly preceding the imposing form of The Wraith.

"Men of the Dragon, hear me now!" The Wraith boomed. "Your days in my city are numbered. Know that I am watching you, watching every move you make, and I will not allow you to turn her into your own personal battlefield."

Tzi's bottom lip quivered and contorted with anger as he listened to every word.

"Your time is coming, Tzi," The Wraith said. "Today marks the beginning of your downfall, and I promise you, neither you nor Robert Latham will come out of this unscathed!"

At this Tzi stood sharply, as though about to reply with a threat of his own, but he stopped himself as The Wraith seemed to almost float backward, unearthly, back into the still-billowing smoke. And in moments, he was gone.

"Find him! No one threatens the Dragon and lives!" Tzi snarled.

Before anyone could move to respond, the room shook to the ferocity of a massive explosion. The lights and monitors flickered briefly before cutting out completely, plunging the room into darkness. The shaking stopped, but panic filled the surveillance room.

"Be calm, be calm," Tzi commanded, but even the Dragon could not control his men's fear. "Find out where that explosion came from."

The men rushed for the door, seemingly ignoring his command, fleeing as fast as they could. Tzi was forced to follow, and he loped through the maze of rooms of his self-styled Chinese paradise toward the house's front door.

Out in the night, what he saw shocked even his jaded eyes. Despite the explosion having taken place a mere two minutes ago, a massive ball of flame was still shooting skyward from where the pool-side bungalow once stood, and through the intense inferno, he could see the gigantic hole through which the flames spewed. Tzi knew at once that his drug lab would never be operational again and he was filled with an anger he had only ever felt once before, back in Hong Kong when his parents had been murdered by English officials when he was just a child. He knew this was the work of The Wraith. He looked up to the barely visible stars and swore vengeance.

* * * * * *

Robert Latham sat at the desk of his eccentrically furnished study, surrounded by the busts of the dictators he so admired—Caesar, Mussolini, Napoleon, George W. Bush and others—as he received news of his forces now retreating from battle.

No matter, he thought, sniffing indignantly, as he listened on the phone. Once finished, he lay the phone back into its cradle. Every incursion he ordered was merely to ascertain weak points in Tzi's armor. Latham knew there were such weak spots, knew they must exist, and was determined to find them no matter the cost or sacrifice. He wasn't about to let some outsider step into his city, meddle with his personal property, and do as he pleased. No, this would not be allowed, and whatever the cost, he would prevail over his newest enemy. If need be, he would fight his war on two fronts—against Tzi and against The Wraith...and he would win.

He turned in his chair and gazed out his large bay window, out onto his lawn, watching the lights of the city glittering in the background. *The city...my city.* He had done much to repair what the Cobra had wrought. In some small way, he felt it his job to make amends to the city which he had helped bring to partial destruction by calling in the Cobra in the first place. In doing so, he not only contributed to the deaths of countless thousands, but that of his own daughter as well. Despite these horrors, strangely, he felt no great sense of remorse, as he deemed them all casualties of war. A war he must win.

He breathed heavily and spun back around to face his desk. Getting back to his paperwork, he began signing several important documents when he heard a tap at his window. He looked up with surprise, and turned to face The Wraith, staring at him through the bay window. Though shocked, Latham didn't budge. The Wraith raised his hand to the window, his fingers pressing against it. With a loud crash, shattered glass showered over Latham and throughout the study. Latham shielded his eyes from the shards.

A thick haze wafted into the study, courtesy of a gas pellet lobbed into the room. Latham coughed and hacked as he brushed the bits of glass from his suit. Blinded by the smoke, he froze, waiting for what he thought would be an inevitable attack. It didn't come. Instead, the familiar booming tone of The Wraith's voice beckoned.

"Latham, your sins against humanity have continued tonight. They will cease, or I will wreck unmitigated harm upon you. You surely realize I speak the truth and are aware of the consequences!"

Latham sputtered as the smoke finally began to dissipate. There was no one to reply to. The Wraith had gone...and Latham was alone.

~ Chapter 2 ~

Leena Patterson stepped through the secret doorway leading from The Wraith's Lair into the Sanderson House study library. The light of the morning sun streamed through the ornate windows, bathing the study in an orange and yellow glow. She flopped down onto the antique brown wing chair. Max followed her from the Lair into the library, which was a superb example of Victorian taste and flavor, with a dash of Art Deco thrown in. The stylish marquetry of the mahogany wood paneling, the lavish carpet, the rich Italian leather of the chairs and sofa, and the walls lined floor-to-ceiling with mahogany bookshelves filled with monographs of innumerable sizes and subjects, all contributed to the sense of class and style that the Sanderson family had long been renowned for prior to the original Paul Sanderson's obsession with privacy. Sanderson had been a lifelong fan of Sherlock Holmes—of the Victorian Era in general—and this room was intended as his sanctuary from the rigors of his life, his 221B Baker Street, where he could not only escape and relax—if only for a short time—but also to sometimes think and plan. A feeling the new Paul Sanderson, naturally, shared. Leena understood this sentiment, and felt the same way. Max now appeared alongside her.

"How long do you think he'll be?" Leena asked.

"The Chief should have been home already," Max responded in his thick Irish brogue. "I hope he didn't have any trouble. Maybe I should have..."

"You did the right thing; you followed orders. And with my impersonating The Wraith at Latham's, we achieved a double impact tonight."

"That we did," Paul said as he exited the Lair through the secret doorway. The sliding bookcase slid back into place with a slight thud. Paul smiled, but looked tired. It had been a hard night's work, and he was visibly exhausted. Since being injured in his battle with the Cobra, he had spent months recovering and undergoing intensive recuperative therapy. Leena knew this inactivity had troubled him, that he had worried the city would be in danger while he wasn't able to patrol the city as The Wraith. Leena and Max had done what they could, and she was, in many ways, as capable and skilled as her partner, but despite this, Ma Tzi had still managed to not only gain a foothold of power within the city, but an almost stranglehold. Ever since being able to resume his duties, Paul had been playing catch up. Leena knew he blamed himself for what had happened and was somehow trying to make it up by working harder, faster, pushing himself ever more. The strain was beginning to show on his body and, behind his eyes, in his mind as well.

"Darling, you look terrible," Leena said, concerned. She stood and lovingly rubbed his cheek.

"I'm okay, I promise," Paul replied, as he sat on the small and comfortable sofa to the side of the antique chair.

Leena sat back down; Max remained standing.

"Tzi get the message?" she asked.

"Mission successful?" asked Max, at the same time.

"Yes to both questions," Paul said. "The explosives worked perfectly, Max. Small but incredibly powerful. Tzi may have to get into another line of business, at least from that location. I doubt even that level of destruction will change his mind though, but the message was well and truly received. Now, how did Latham react to your warning, Leena?"

"Knowing Latham, he was furious and ready to take revenge. But at least they both know we mean business. And your padded suit, Max, worked to perfection." Max smiled at this. "Latham had no idea he wasn't dealing with the true Wraith."

Paul stood. "Good. I intend to shut them both down—for good." He looked as determined as he sounded as he walked slowly out of the library.

Leena and Max looked to each other and she wondered what Paul had planned, wondered if it were indeed possible to do as he stated.

"Why don't you go to bed and I'll talk with Paul," Leena suggested.

Max nodded his agreement.

Leena found Paul in the kitchen and joined him at the small kitchen nook the couple used for their morning breakfast. Paul was drinking a cup of Earl Grey tea, and motioned for Leena to join him.

"Are you sure you're all right? You look exhausted and I'm not sure you're making sense about shutting Latham and Tzi down completely."

Paul smiled weakly. "You don't think it can be done? You don't think I can achieve this?"

"No, that's not what I'm saying, but...you know you're not fully recovered yet. I just think it's too soon to be making such promises."

Paul seemed to be listening intently as he poured her a cup of tea. "I can't let the two of them destroy this city. Their war has gone on long enough and tonight marked the beginning of the end—*their* end."

Leena looked at the love of her life with concern, but knew not to press him any further. Paul had fully meant what he said and she knew if anyone could achieve this goal, he could. And she intended to be there every step of the way, in whatever capacity he needed.

She placed her head on his shoulder. "Get some rest, darling. I've got to shower and get ready for work." She stood, smiled at him, and exited the kitchen.

* * * * * *

Her voice made his body tingle. Every time. He loved her so much and he hoped everyday she knew just how much. Paul sipped the last drops of tea from his cup then stood. He knew that while he had made his desired impact tonight, this was truly only the beginning. As he made his way toward the door, he suddenly felt a sense of foreboding.

Yes, he thought, *this is only the beginning.*

* * * * * *

Peter Smith was a good, honest man in his mid-thirties. He had a fine job with a leading accounting firm, was happily married with two small children, and was well liked by colleagues and friends. He was the kind of man Metro City sorely needed, but had very little of.

As he did every weekday morning, Smith set off for work by walking from his inner city apartment to the nearest subway station, about two blocks away at the corner of Fifth and Elm Street. While a milky, weak sun strained to pierce through today's polluted Metro City sky, Smith looked up and smiled. He had always thought to himself that if he could make it in a hellhole like Metro City, he could make it anywhere. The thought always brightened his mood despite his surroundings. He had grown up in Metro City, and in spite of its steep decline in the ensuing years, he was loathe to move. A terrible city it may have become, but underneath it all, he still believed in this city, believed he could somehow make a difference albeit in his own small way.

As he made his way along the bustling crowded street, he suddenly felt a twinge in his throat, a tickling sensation. He coughed, and while the feeling hadn't vanished, he thought nothing more of it, concentrating on making the 8:35 A.M. train instead. Looking at his watch, he picked up his pace. Reaching the stairway entrance to the station, he sprang down the steps two at a time. His train was approaching the platform as he thrust his token into the gates and hustled toward the now opening train door.

Plunking himself into a vacant seat near the door, he realized he was sweating profusely, something he almost never did without the most intense exertion. Confused, he wiped his brow. Was he coming down with something? Obviously, he was normally blessed with the kind of health everyone who knew him was envious of. As his thoughts whirled, he realized his breathing had increased, as though he had just played his brother in their usual Wednesday evening racquetball match. And the tickling in his throat had grown, causing him to involuntarily cough in a vain attempt to quell the irritation.

"Hey, you don't look so good," said the young man who was sitting next to him and who was now beginning to move slowly away.

"I—I don't know what's wrong with me," hacked Smith, trying to make sense of what was happening and to make his throat irritation disappear. "I was fine just a few minutes ago."

"Yeah, well, you're not fine anymore," said the young man, who stood and began walking away.

"My...my name's Peter Smith...I need some help," he gasped. He began coughing more furiously, and couldn't seem to clear his throat. The coughing escalated into intense heaving. His skin began to crawl and he felt hot and cold at the same time. His clothes were drenched with sweat, and when blood appeared in his sputum, he knew he was in serious trouble.

* * * * * *

Smith lurched to his feet. "Help me," he gurgled before collapsing. The train leaned into a sharp bend, turning a corner. The nearby commuters screamed in horror at the devastating sight before them. Peter Smith lay there, his skin blotched in what appeared to be dreadful, glistening crimson welts. A puddle indicated he had wet himself as he fell. As the commuters scrambled to escape the horror, Smith lay there, prone...dead!

* * * * * *

The Metro City Library, where Leena worked as the Reference Librarian, was busier than usual today. Already one of the most visited libraries in the country—with anywhere between three and five thousand visitors daily—today seemed just one of those days where every enquiry needed a detailed response, requiring the time and effort to extract just the right answer needed by each individual patron. Questions about Olympic Games athletes Leena had never heard of, details of Greek mythology, the geography of a district of Tasmania in Australia, and the history of literature in Lithuania ensured her morning was a most intense one.

In the staff room, having survived to her morning break, Leena sipped from her cup of coffee and tried to remember the last time it was this busy. She couldn't. Peering around for a magazine to peruse in the few minutes respite she had, the manager, Astrid, appeared for her break, looking a little worse for wear. Normally of a bright and cheery disposition, with short cropped blonde hair, Astrid this morning looked anything but.

"You don't look any better, Astrid. If anything, you look worse," Leena said candidly. She and Astrid were good friends and close colleagues. She had been there for Leena when Michael Reeve, her boyfriend, had "died." Leena had really appreciated that, more than she'd ever told her. Little did anyone know that Michael had in fact not only survived, but in some fantastic way she still didn't fully comprehend, he had somehow become two men in one—Michael Reeve *and* Paul Sanderson. The reclusive millionaire, Sanderson, had proven to be the mysterious Wraith, the vigilante that prowled the Metro City nights, attacking evil like a cancer. And now Reeve lived his life as Sanderson and The Wraith, choosing the path of righteousness and justice, Leena by his side.

"Thanks, you're a great help," Astrid said. She began coughing a little.

Leena looked on, worried. Astrid really didn't look well at all. "I don't think you're well enough to stay on. I know we're busy today, but we can still cope without you for a day or two." She sat beside Astrid, placing her hand to her forehead. "Lord, you're burning up. You're actually hot to the touch."

Astrid squirmed in her seat, vainly trying to get comfortable. She was now sweating strongly and her coughing had increased. Leena knew something was gravely wrong and managed to catch Astrid as she pitched out of her chair.

"Somebody call an ambulance!" Leena screamed. A coworker quickly appeared at the staffroom door and almost panicked at the sight of Astrid prostrate in Leena's arms on the floor.

"Quickly, call an ambulance," Leena ordered. Normally Leena was well trained for extreme situations such as this. The mate of the Dread Avenger of the Underworld could be no less. Before Paul would agree to let Leena remain a part of his life, he insisted she undergo a rigorous training regimen, one to match his own. Thus, she was now an expert hand-to-hand combatant, trained to near physical perfection in martial arts, weaponry, gymnastics and criminology, as well as first aid. Even so, she found herself in a position she never dreamed possible, and barely contained her emotions as her manager—her friend—lay dying in her arms.

It was over in minutes. Leena gently set Astrid's head on the floor and, with no thought for her own safety, mopped up Astrid's blotched face with a handkerchief as best she could before covering the corpse with her jacket. Inside, she was reeling. One of her closest friends had just perished, horribly. Yet, her training held firm, and she remained strong and in control. The Wraith had taught her well.

She exited the staff room, almost staggering for the library's front entrance. She needed air, needed space away from her colleagues, needed to think things through. *What just happened in there?* Her mind raced with all kinds of thoughts. *Could this mean...?*

Her thoughts were interrupted by the sight of people in the street, maybe a half dozen or so, collapsing, coughing, bleeding, excreting—violently, shockingly. Despite her training, Leena felt nauseous at what was transpiring before her, but she somehow managed to control herself. She knew she had to alert the authorities, and Paul. The possibility she had briefly raised mere moments ago were now confirmed as her worst fears evidenced before her.

A plague had infected Metro City.

~ Chapter 3 ~

In an immense black room, where the light was dim and red, a provocatively-dressed woman sat upon a grand throne of skulls. A small, sinister smile curled upon her full, red lips. Her deputy, Magnus Khan, stood nearby.

"The operation goes well," she purred.

Khan, a bearded man dressed in the loose wrappings and armored wrist guards of an ancient Mongolian warrior, stopped abruptly. "You know?"

"I know nothing except that my own plan was flawless." She stood and moved slowly toward Khan. Her long, straight brown hair tumbled down, partially covering her plunging décolletage. Her blue-green eyes sparkled with a heady mix of intelligence and beauty, and the intensity of her gaze bespoke of harshness and cruelty. Her skintight outfit, revealing as it was, set off the slight tan of her beautiful skin, which held perhaps the merest suggestion of Levantine blood generations before her family moved to Russia. "The citizens of Metro City are feeling my wrath. The plague is beginning to take hold. Many thousands will die before my vengeance is satisfied. Then I will take what is rightfully mine in the name of our great master." Khan's gaze followed her as she ambled toward the door at the far end of the room. "The city will tremble at the names Cobra and Natalya Blackova, and I will conquer all who stand in my way!" With Khan at her heels, the former KGB operative continued. "Ready the next batch of plague. I want the city to suffer before I am ready to make my next move."

"Yes, my Mistress." Khan parted company with Blackova and he knew her lascivious smile would return in anticipation of the death and destruction wrought in her name.

* * * * * *

Leena moved through the open bookcase doorway leading from the library to the Lair. The Lair, a massive open-plan sanctum, architecturally a mix of the futuristic and Art Deco, was segmented into sections in which computers, a gym, laboratory and costumes were located. It was the Lair that was the true headquarters of The Wraith, where he trained, worked. She had rushed home as quickly as possible after being delayed by the authorities requiring a statement. As she went down in the open, oval elevator, she could see Paul huddled at the massive computer terminal located at the Lair's center. She quickly joined him and knew he was already well aware of the plague's outbreak upon the city.

"Reports have been coming in all day from all my contacts. Best estimates indicate hundreds dead, and from the look of the virulence of this plague, we could see thousands in quick time."

Leena looked into Paul's fevered face. She knew what this was doing to him. This city and its people meant everything to him. Everything he did, everything he was, was for the benefit of Metro City. She knew well the turmoil racing within him, and she knew that he was probably the city's only hope.

Paul glanced up at her. "I'm sorry, darling. Are you okay? I know Astrid was a friend."

She frowned, on the verge of tears. "It was dreadful. The end came so quickly. I've never felt so helpless." She paused, on the cusp of losing it. She regained her composure.

Paul stood and took her in his arms. "I'm so sorry, darling. But we don't have time to mourn. A plague like this doesn't appear out of nowhere, with no warning. And from the reports coming in, this is unlike any virus we've ever seen. The hand of man is involved, without doubt."

Leena reached into her pocket and pulled out a vial filled with a flaky, reddish substance. "I took some skin samples. I knew you'd want to take a closer look."

Paul eagerly took the vial and rushed over to the Lair's laboratory, a lab Sanderson money ensured was the best in the state, if not the country. Soon, he was hunched over a variety of microscopes, scanners and test tubes, working feverishly in Max's absence, the true scientific brains of the team, trying to obtain answers—the plague's origins, virulence or anything else that could be discovered.

"From the looks of things, I think we've all been exposed, including myself, so isolation seems pointless," Leena said as she intently watched him work. He seemed to have not heard her.

"This is unlike anything I've ever seen. Nothing like Ebola or Bubonic Plague. The skin appears melted, as though burned by an intense heat. The blood that oozed from the welts actually boiled upon contact with the air. Take a look." He motioned for her to come and look through the microscope.

"You're right," she replied after having peered through the lens. "You can clearly see the evidence of incredible heat. How is that possible?"

"I don't know," he said. "Max may be able to tell us more when he returns. We have to know what we're dealing with here."

Paul sat back down and continued with his chemical analysis. Leena placed a hand on his shoulder, concerned about him and for the city.

She looked around. "Where is Max?"

"He hasn't returned yet from his duties in the city—" His words broke off as soon as he said them.

Leena saw the concern in his face, and she felt the same way. She hoped Max was safe and well.

* * * * * *

Max had exited his favorite tobacco store on Sixth Street when he saw events that made his breakfast start to rear up in his throat. People were dropping to the pavement, heaving, bleeding, dying. To even a battle-hardened warrior such as he, the sight appalled him. He turned and raced back into the store, intending to phone the authorities and, of course, the Dread Avenger of the Underworld. What he saw once he entered chilled him to the bone. The store's proprietor, Richard Jones, a good friend of his, was convulsing over the cash register, his breathing labored, hideous pustules of blood and blistered flesh appearing over his face and hands.

"Rich!" Max raced behind the counter just in time to catch him as Jones experienced one final, violent seizure, and keeled over backward. Max cradled him gently in his arms and held him for what seemed an eternity. He looked at the almost unrecognizable face of his now-dead friend. The pustules on his friends face were bubbling as though volcanic magma had burst through his flesh. The smell of blood and puss turned his stomach inside out. He gently laid the body down on the shop floor then shakily managed to stand.

He remained there almost in a trance before moving out into the street, completely forgetting about the phone. His years of training took hold and he carefully and cautiously scanned the area around him. He estimated a good quarter of the people were afflicted by this terrible disease. It had to be a sickness of some sort. What else could he call it? The sidewalks on both sides of the street were littered with bodies; people huddled around the dead. There were screams of torment, terror and unmatched pain. Panic was beginning to envelope the city in its deadly grasp.

Max thought, *If roughly a quarter of the population has been affected and that figure repeated throughout the city, the number of deaths would number at least...* Max stopped himself. The figures that raced through his brain were too horrendous to even contemplate, and the realization of so many potential deaths made him feel ill.

And then, he saw something that sent shivers down his spine. *There, across the street. The alley.* He blinked. In that split-second, it was gone. Without hesitation, Max rushed across the street, toward the alley, and entered its inky recesses.

~ Chapter 4 ~

Commissioner George Harrison, an honest cop in a city that didn't have much time for honesty, exploded from his office. "Sloan! Perez!" he screamed. "Get in here!"

Detective Bob Sloan, a burly man in his fifties with pug-nosed features, and his partner, Rosa Perez, a pretty, but tough-looking Latina woman, quickly responded.

"We've got the National Guard coming in to cordon off the city. No one goes in or out. So far, there are no reports of this...plague...affecting anyone else in the state or the country. So, that's the good news." Harrison paused for a moment. "The bad news is we don't know just yet how many have died. Numbers could hit the thousands. And we don't know what we're dealing with yet and how contagious it may be, though we've seen ample evidence of its virulence."

Harrison, a short, rotund man with a thinning head of hair but a full, bushy mustache, moved over to his office window and peered through the blinds into the busy workspace his officers filled. Busy as it was, dealing with the day's horrendous slaughter, it was nevertheless emptier than usual. Sloan knew what that potentially meant, and the thought chilled him even more.

"The National Lab boys are on their way, surely?" Sloan said.

"They'll be here as soon as possible and we have our own team working on this as best we can," Harrison said. "We don't know what incubation period this virus has, if any, but we know the entire city has somehow been exposed. Just how it's been exposed, we don't know yet." He sighed. "What I do know is, is that I want you two on this. I don't care what it takes or how you do it, but find out all you can. Viruses like this just don't pop out of nowhere. This could be an external terrorist attack; we have the Feds looking into that theory. In the meantime, if it's some local psycho, I want to know and I want them caught. Now!"

Harrison turned and rounded his desk. Perez eyed Sloan gravely. "So, where do we begin?" she asked.

"Morgue," Sloan answered. "We need to see Howard. There may not be any answers yet, but at this stage I'll be happy to deal with some informed theories. Come on."

* * * * * *

Max strode cautiously through the darkened alleyway. He didn't want to advertise his presence just yet and wanted the potential for surprise. Navigating the strewn garbage cans and open sewer outfall, he soon arrived at the entrance to a large, rounded cul-de-sac. He stopped at the corner and carefully peered around it. At the far end of the cul-de-sac, was a large parked van. Magnus Khan entered its side door. Max recognized him all too well based on The Wraith's description of him—long-haired and bearded, Khan looked for all the world like an ancient Mongolian warlord. Khan's presence here, at that time, sounded alarm bells in Max's head. *Khan—or the Cobra?—could they be responsible for this plague?* The possibility was a strong one.

Khan slid the door shut and for a few minutes the van remained parked there, no sign of life from those inside. Max stayed in hiding, not wishing to come out in the open, but not yet knowing what to do next. Then, the van roared to life, and inched forward, toward Max's vantage point. The exit to the cul-de-sac was located around the corner to his left. He had to think fast. As the car slowly moved past him, he leaped out and attached a small locater device to the rear of the car. He didn't have time to properly hide it, but it was fastened solidly, and would enable him to be able to ascertain Khan's movements before reporting to home base.

As the van vanished into city traffic, Max raced to the nearby Daimler parked two blocks away.

I can't let Khan get away again, he thought. He got behind the Daimler's wheel and gunned the engine, spinning the wheels, and hurried in pursuit of the van.

* * * * * *

At the City Morgue, attendants rushed about, trying to make sense of the senseless. Bodies lay everywhere, many of them not covered, all of them in appalling condition, with horrific orange and red hued pustules and mottled skin. The smell of charred flesh and excrement caused Perez to cover her nose and mouth; a feeling of nausea began to nearly overwhelm her. As she and her partner inched through the chaos, she turned to Sloan, whose expression portrayed both anger and incredible sadness. Chief Medical Examiner Howard Boynce, a tall and thin man with penetrating eyes behind thin glasses and a bouffant hairstyle, appeared from his office. Upon spotting the two detectives, he came toward them.

"We've run out of space, as you can see," Boynce said. Perez noticed he was clearly exhausted and wondered if he could hold out the day let alone until this disaster was resolved. "The city hospitals are experiencing the same." He paused briefly. "We've even run out of material to cover these poor souls." He put his hands to his face.

"Easy, Howard, easy," said Sloan.

Boynce sighed. "It's just this feeling of helplessness. The speed at which this virus operates is phenomenal. I honestly don't know if there's anything we can do to fight it."

Sloan and Perez eyed each other with concern. Finally, Sloan broke the silence. "Howard, I know this thing's a complete mystery to everyone so far, especially at this early stage, but I need something, anything. A thought, a theory, a guess—something."

Howard sighed again then stepped over to the nearest corpse. "Take this poor fellow. Look at his skin." Boynce prodded carefully on the dead man's cheek. As horrific as the sight was, Sloan and Perez bent down to watch Boynce make his point. "His skin clearly appears burned. Look at the texture, there are classic burn marks mixed in with those horrible contusions. And yet, there's been no evidence of any flame being involved with these deaths. These look much more like chemical burns, but again, there's been no evidence thus far obtained indicating a chemical agent being involved."

"So what do you make of that?" Sloan said, his face clouded over with confusion.

"I don't know. With what little I have to work with here, I can't find anything out myself. I have a thought or two, but...we'll have to wait for the National Lab people to arrive onsite."

Sloan appeared impatient. "Howard. Give. I need something to go on here."

Boynce turned and shuffled toward his office, with Sloan and Perez following close behind.

"Howard?" Perez asked softly.

"I don't know. This is pure guesswork, you understand, but it's an idea I can't get out of my head–maybe it's possible someone was able to mix an Ebola-like virus with a form of Napalm, or something very much like Napalm." Sloan eyed Boynce with incredulity. "I know, it sounds crazy, and yet" –he pointed to the countless dead surrounding them– "there you have it. Like I said, I'm only guessing, and it's not something I would have thought possible until I saw these people with my own eyes."

"Okay," Sloan said, the three of them now in Boynce's cramped and cluttered office. "Say you're right, say this is something as you describe. Then how do we fight it? And who would be able to create something of this power *and* on this scale?"

"Like I said, this is totally beyond my capabilities. This could very well be a terrorist attack. Let's face it, we're not exactly beloved beyond our borders. Look at the world today, take your pick of enemies. I'm sure there are several options out there. And I'm also sure the Feds are well aware of the situation and are assessing their own theories, for all the good that does us right now. I severely doubt this is a local threat though, Detective." Boynce's beeper interrupted the trio, and the medical examiner quickly excused himself.

"I'm not so sure, Perez. I think this could be a local sicko," said Sloan as they exited the office and were back amongst the sickening multitude of casualties.

"How can you say that?" she said. "We have no evidence to back that up. The immenseness of this plague has to indicate an outside source. I think the terrorist angle is the most likely right now."

"Is it? I'm not so sure. You're right. We don't have anything to go on, but I have my gut instinct, and it's rarely let me down."

The two left the building and made their way toward their parked car. The streets were empty (the authorities had ordered people to stay home, the only safety they could think of for folks to not be infected by the plague). Perez thanked God that the authorities had gotten to this section of the city and removed the bodies. The same could not be said for many other parts of the city though. She ruminated on this, and the ghost town Metro City had become, and quickly realized the enormity of the task before them.

* * * * * *

Traffic was incredibly sparse—not surprising with the disaster now enveloping the city. Emergency vehicles would appear from time to time, and the amount of dead on the sidewalks and streets still made Max seethe with anger, but he had another task at hand. The scanner located within the center console of the classic Daimler he was driving beeped with a constant flicker of activity as he tracked the van through the heart of the city. He lingered a safe distance back. He knew with traffic being next to nothing, any closer would surely signal his presence to his quarry. And what a quarry. Magnus Khan, the powerful deputy to the Cobra, the greatest evil this city—and The Wraith—had ever faced. *Does this mean the Cobra survived his fall?* The thought raced through Max's mind, and it both chilled and enraged the Irishman.

He veered the Daimler out of the central business district and into and through the inner city suburbs of Gladstone, Surry Hills and Aubcombe. *Where are they be headed?* he wondered. They were indeed leading him on a merry chase, but he felt confident his presence was still unknown to his enemies. *How could they detect me at least two miles back?*

As the density of the suburbs began to lessen, Max continued with his pursuit. The chase had thus far lasted well over an hour and he wondered just how long it would go on. Just as the thought vanished, an answer of a sort appeared in his rear-view mirror. The van he had been trailing all this time was now behind him—and catching up fast. Yet his radar continued to indicate the van was in front of him. Having no time to think about how it was possible, for his quarry was now rearing up behind him, he jammed his foot down hard on the gas, increasing his speed. The van instantly did likewise. Though the Daimler was thoroughly modernized beneath the hood—courtesy of his own tinkering—and capable of great speeds, he soon found the van was up to the task and was gaining on him.

"Dammit!" he muttered. "This was a trap, and I fell for it like an amateur."

Tires screeched as he violently gripped the wheel, barely succeeding in negotiating a sharp corner to his left in an attempt to shake his pursuers. The van managed to follow suit without losing an inch from the chase. Both cars hurtled through the thin roadblock set up by the authorities that afternoon. Max realized the reason for it, but could do little else. The chase was on. The van was tail-gating the Daimler with surprising ease. The van nudged the Daimler's rear bumper, causing the car—and Max—to lurch forward.

"I can't shake these guys no matter what I do," he groaned, while doing everything he could—everything he could think of—to take back the advantage. Nothing worked. The van slipped alongside the Daimler's right, further playing this dangerous game of cat and mouse. Max craned his neck to his right as best and as quickly as he could, but the van's windows were heavily tinted so the occupants other than Khan were still a mystery.

Both vehicles continued screaming down the street at top speed, having reached a semi-rural area deserted of major traffic. What cars there were could clearly see the danger approaching them; they moved out of the way to avoid it. Max was running out of options. He had been confident of the superiority of his own vehicle, of his own skills even, but those notions had been shattered as nothing more than an illusion. He was barely keeping control of the car.

The van careened into the Daimler's side, causing him to nearly lose control. The Daimler crashing up onto the grassy curb, scraping along a barbed wire fence, partially destroying the fence in the process. Max grimaced at the sickening sound of metal grating on metal (and also at the amount of damage being done to his beloved car). The van repeated the move and again he struggled to stay in control at such a high speed.

"Dammit!" Max said. He tried valiantly to fight back, to do the same to the van, but despite the strength and power of the Daimler, the size and strength of the van limited his endeavors. Still side-by-side with the van, Max worried at the outcome of this deadly struggle. He quickly thought to press a small button on his console, a signal to The Wraith of his location, lest worse come to worse. He cursed himself that he hadn't contacted the Chief back in the city when he'd had the opportunity. It was too late, and he too harried, to cry over spilled milk.

The sun was beginning to set over the looming escarpment, drenching the countryside and the two desperate combatants in a gorgeous orange hue that belied the struggle now taking place. Fast approaching a dilapidated church, the van made its final move, brutally bashing into the Daimler with incredible vigor, sending Max twisting off-road and crashing headfirst into the side of the decaying old church in a cacophony of rending metal, crumbling sandstone and billowing smoke.

Once the dust had settled, Magnus Khan appeared and opened the Daimler's driver's side door. Max was barely conscious though uninjured; his body partially hung out of the car. Thankfully, the airbag had saved his life. He looked up through misty eyes. Khan grinned at him with malice.

"Everything is going according to plan," Khan said, as his men, clad in ninja-like garb, joined him. "Take him. Phase Three now begins."

~ Chapter 5 ~

Paul sat in the Lair's laboratory, still analyzing the skin sample Leena had taken, anxious to determine as much as he could about the virus that had swept through his city with such apparent—and lethal—ease. He was so lost in his research he hadn't heard her come in, nor had he heard her take the elevator down to join him.

She had been standing behind him for several minutes before she spoke. "Any word from Max?"

"Hmm...oh, not yet," Paul replied slowly.

"I'm worried about him. It's not like him to stay away this long without reporting in. You know him and his habits."

Paul took a moment before replying. "Max can take care of himself, darling. I know how you feel, but we have more important problems to deal with right now." He saw her brow furrow over with concern.

"Have you uncovered anything?" she asked.

Paul straightened, finally removing himself from his microscope and test tubes. "My contact at the City Morgue alerted me to a theory of Howard Boynce's, and I think he's on the right track."

"Meaning?"

"This isn't Ebola, that much we could establish early. But it does show certain qualities of that virus. I think it's a genetically altered strain, a unique combination of Ebola and something else, something I haven't yet been able to determine. But the ingenuity of this is the Napalm additive."

Her voice rose a pitch. "Napalm?"

"Or something very much like it. That's what produces those burn marks on the skin of the victims. Just how they were able to blend such a concoction together to create such a powerful agent of death...I honestly don't know."

Leena took this all in with stern concentration. "Despite the incredible amount of dead, why aren't more of us contracting the virus? From the various reports we've gotten, and from my own observations, it seems so...calculated somehow...almost like a set number of people have been targeted. I know that sounds crazy. How's that even possible?"

Paul stood. "Leena, you've got it. This isn't a virus at all, at least not in the way we think. The amount of dead had us all confused. It's not contagious at all."

"You mean—these are a case of mass poisonings?"

"No, not quite. This *is* a virus. Radically altered at a genetic level from what I can tell, but still a virus. But it's not contagious as such." He strode from his workstation and began to pace up-and-down the Lair's intricate lab. "So, it's obviously administered to the victims somehow, and on a massive scale. There must be some common element then between all the victims, some aspect that links them all. If we can discover that, we'll know how this virus was spread."

"But a cure?" Leena asked.

"If we can learn the method of dissemination, and control and stop it, we'll negate the immediate need for a cure. We can then—" He was interrupted by a loud buzzing from his computer console. Paul rushed over to answer the incoming signal. "It's the Daimler's emergency beacon. Max is in trouble."

Leena quickly followed him toward the wall where he stored his costumes.

"The signal came from Regency Heights, near the escarpment," Paul said, removing portions of The Wraith costume from a stand. "Get that information to Commissioner Harrison. Now that we have a better idea of what we're dealing with, you can work together to find the method of diffusion and put an end to this horror."

"And what about you?"

"I'll determine what's happened with Max."

* * * * * *

In the darkened study Latham considered his sanctuary, he sat at his desk, engaged in a heated conversation over the phone. His demeanor was almost fevered—and certainly passionate—as he attempted to hold his business empire together through a massive gang war and now the city's great plague.

"Yes, let me assure you that business will resume as soon as the current crisis is over," Latham stated firmly. "No, this is *not* the final straw. Ma Tzi is under control, and this crisis will soon be also." He paused as he listened. And grimaced.

"I do not accept that; I do not accept your termination of our agreement. The arrangement we have can only be terminated by *me*, do you understand?" He paused again. "I will say this once more: business will resume as soon as this crisis is over. I will brook no more talk of otherwise!" He slammed the phone back on its cradle.

He swiveled in his chair to find his deputy, Charlie Grieco, standing in the open door.

"How long have you been standing there?" asked Latham, still agitated.

"Long enough." Grieco was a younger, slicker version of Latham, with intelligence and energy to burn. What he also had was an appetite for power, one which oftentimes clouded his better judgment. "Was that the Afghans?"

Latham sighed. "Yes, but I have the situation under control."

Grieco took a few steps inside the room, a look of smarmy pleasure on his face. Latham wondered if Grieco was actually enjoying this, enjoying seeing him in trouble.

"Are you sure? Sounds to me like they're running scared," Grieco said.

"Everything is under control, Charlie. Business will resume in due course, and I won't let this plague, Ma Tzi or anyone else stop me from re-building my empire."

"Yes, Mr. Latham. I just hope there's an empire left to rebuild."

Grieco turned and ambled casually out of the office. Latham pondered his deputy's statement.

* * * * * *

Commissioner Harrison looked up at the night sky. It was a crystal clear night, and the sky looked incredibly beautiful, he thought. One could almost be lost within the Milky Way's nebulous strands, endlessly ruminating over life and one's own place in it, but he was brought back to Earth by a strong voice sinking in volume but rising in intensity.

"The plague. I have information."

Harrison whirled to see The Wraith standing in the darkness at the far end of the roof, partially hidden by the building's rooftop chimney.

"We could use some. We haven't come up with anything, and the Feds are still mobilizing," Harrison said.

The Wraith remained perfectly still in the darkness, the light shining toward Harrison helping to obscure his view of the Dread Avenger of the Underworld.

"The plague isn't contagious; it's administered by some outside agent," The Wraith said.

Harrison sucked in a large breathe of air, shocked by this revelation. "But how can that be?"

"I need your help," The Wraith said, ignoring the question. He tossed to the floor a manila folder. "Take that. Evidence backing up what I've said. We need to find out what the victims had in common. There must be some common element that links them all together. They might have all visited the same restaurant, all received the same junk mail, used the same conditioner—something that ties them all together. You have to put your entire resources behind this search. Only then can we discover how the virus was spread and how we can contain it."

"It's a massive task. I don't know..."

"It must be done! This is the only way we can stop the virus in its tracks and save this city."

"Yes, yes, of course," Harrison said. "It will be done." He turned, shut his eyes, clutched the bridge of his nose and sighed with the strain of the job, especially under the current circumstances. "I don't know how to...thank you." He returned his gaze toward The Wraith, but found himself once again alone on the rooftop, the breeze and the stars his only companions.

* * * * * *

The Daimler was a write-off. The Wraith could see that the instant he arrived at the scene. He had driven there post haste, managing to slide by the still-thin barrier of the police. The beacon, only used in the strongest of emergencies, worked perfectly, indicating the exact location of the wreck. The Wraith examined it carefully for any clues to Max's location. There was no blood visible, so he was confident Max was not badly hurt. Max had obviously been found, most likely taken hostage, for Max would never have let himself be taken except if he were waylaid by a trap. The identity of the kidnappers and where Max might have been taken, however, was a mystery.

As The Wraith was about to turn back to his own car, he stopped, something catching the corner of his eye. It was a small piece of vegetation lying just outside the wrecked driver's side door. He carefully picked it up and looked at it closely.

An odd color, he thought.

Nothing around the old church matched it. And yet, it somehow appeared familiar to him, something about the color, the texture. He quickly produced a powerful magnifying glass from his belt and scrutinized the specimen.

Then, he remembered. It was a rare species of tree, only recently re-discovered after scientists had long since thought it extinct. A Neolithic survivor of a bygone age. And the only place where the species remained was a hidden valley over the escarpment. Hidden to all except National Park's representatives. And The Wraith.

He raced back to the Bentley Continental GT he often drove as Paul Sanderson, and geared the sports car back into the street. His mind raced with ideas. He could drive there, but the distance was still a long one, and the valley itself remote and inaccessible by vehicular traffic. No, the best way was by air. He couldn't waste valuable time going back for his own plane, and he knew there was a small airstrip nearby where a plane could be commandeered. At the next intersection, The Wraith gunned his car to the left, and made haste toward his objective.

At high speed, the airstrip appeared within minutes. Despite the hour, he recognized the facility by the array of lights, and turned into the drive before screeching to a halt before the strip's only building, a medium-sized hangar. The Wraith ran inside, past a bewildered, elderly security officer, toward the only plane left in residence—an aged, though well kept, Northrup. The Dread Avenger leapt aboard, reaching to hotwire the controls before the elderly gentleman, shouting and waving before him, caused any further difficulty. The craft sputtered to life, and The Wraith took the controls with sure hands. An experienced pilot, he had made sure in the past to gain experience in planes of all shapes, sizes and age, and quickly maneuvered the plane past the irate security officer and out into the field that classified as this country suburb's airstrip.

As quickly as possible, The Wraith piloted the craft down the grassy runway, building up speed. He was airborne within moments. The plane was surprisingly agile and well-conditioned. He blessed the fates for allowing him to find such a machine, and aimed it in the direction of the escarpment. Despite the inky blackness of the night, for in spite of the clear sky, no moon was visible. The Dread Avenger knew the area like no other (he made it his business to know this and all else as much as possible). The wind whipped around the craft ferociously as the night breeze had begun to pick up the higher he ascended.

As he wondered of the progress Leena had made tonight with her meeting—impersonating The Wraith—with Commissioner Harrison, an incoming call came through on his cowl radio. He reached up with his right hand and clicked a point at his temple.

"Yes, Leena," he said. He waited. "Good. Harrison's men will no doubt discover the source and make efforts to deal with it." He waited for her response. "I have an idea where Max has been taken. I'll let you know more as soon as I'm able." With that, he switched the radio off with a second tap at his temple, and pushed the Northrup faster toward the approaching mountain range.

* * * * * *

Sloan and Perez, both exhausted, entered their workroom back at Police Headquarters. They had seen enough death and carnage in one night to last them a lifetime, and sleep had not come easily. The next morning had not brought any miraculous cheer, and while both were determined to make progress in their investigation, neither had any idea where to go next. Sloan bypassed his desk and headed straight for Commissioner Harrison's office. Perez followed closely behind. Sloan knocked at the open door and both detectives entered.

"Good," Harrison said. "I was about to call you guys. We've got a break in the plague situation." Sloan noticed Harrison looked just as exhausted as Perez did, but was obviously running on the energy of having gotten some answers.

"What? How?" he asked. *Finally, some answers.*

"Never mind. The point is, we have a lead," Harrison said. "I've called the Feds, and while the cordon around the city will remain for now, there isn't any risk of contagion beyond Metro."

Sloan was having trouble taking it all in in his tired state. "Whoa, back up there. No risk of contagion? I don't understand."

"We've discovered the virus isn't contagious per sé. It's administered somehow but only to a select group, and that's where you come in." Harrison threw a manila folder onto his desk for them to see. "Here's the evidence. We need as many men as we can spare on this. Find out what the victims have in common. Did they all eat in the same restaurant, go see the same ballgame, use the same brand of shampoo? Find out, then we'll have our answers."

Recognition emerged on Perez's face. "I get it. That's why the death rate has stabilized now, why we all haven't come down with the virus. Brilliant."

Sloan's gaze moved from Perez back to Harrison. He eyed him strongly. "You got this from The Wraith, didn't you?"

"I did," the commissioner said without hesitation. "It was the break we needed, and we have the potential to save untold lives with this information. Now get going. We need to find that common element and shut whatever it is down."

Sloan knew this wasn't the time to argue about The Wraith. Lives were still at stake, and action was needed. "Come on, Perez. We need to move."

* * * * * *

Ma Tzi sat at his desk in his control room like a monarch lording over his subjects. Despite the plague that had wiped out thousands in the city in such a short amount of time, the Hong Kong businessman had insisted his men remain at their posts as much as was possible during this ordeal. There was still much work to be done repairing the equipment wrecked from The Wraith's attack, and plans needed to be made to replace the inventory destroyed in the underground storage facility.

As Tzi watched his men at work repairing and replacing the intricate electronics in the room, he received a call at the phone beside him. "Yes? Oh really? This will be most interesting. Please send him in." In moments, Charlie Grieco was admitted into the room. None of Tzi's men averted their gaze from their work.

"Mr. Grieco, this is a pleasant surprise. Mr. Latham's right-hand man, it is an honor to receive you. How may I be of service?"

Grieco appeared to attempt to look as confident and tall as possible. He was outfitted in a splendid Italian suit sans tie, and polished Italian leather shoes. "I can see you're a man of the future, like myself. I can also pick a winning team—and this is a winning team." He indicated around him with a wave of his hand.

"You flatter me," Tzi said, smiling briefly. "Go on."

"Robert Latham has lost sight of the core foundations of the business. He's letting his vendettas cloud his judgment.

He's going down in flames and I don't want to go along for the ride."

Tzi stood, ambled over to Grieco, his genteel smile never leaving his face. "What you are really saying is, you wish to have power and you sense a weakness now in Latham that you are willing to exploit, in exchange for assistance from me. Is that not so, Mr. Grieco?"

"I-I..."

"Please, Mr. Grieco, take a seat." Tzi motioned to a chair. "The reason for your being here is immaterial. You have realized that our war can only end one way: the annihilation of Latham's empire and then assimilation with my own. You have foresight to go along with your hunger for power. I can see that. I can see that you wish a smooth transition of power and a better hierarchy of succession for yourself. Let us sit and discuss this matter. I think I can help you achieve *all* your goals."

* * * * * *

As the morning sun began to loom over the horizon, The Wraith piloted the Northrup over the wilderness of the escarpment, watching both his instruments and the surrounding landscape to find both the correct location he was searching for, but also for the nearest place where he could land. The wind had picked up in the time since takeoff and the small, but sturdy, craft was making tough going of the journey. The Wraith gripped the controls with hands of steel. Then, from the corner of his eye, he espied the area, the valley, which was the fruit of his exertions. He turned to get a better look.

Yes, this is the place.

The valley stretched out beneath him, surrounded by immense, sheer cliff faces on all sides that would be difficult —if not impossible—to traverse at speed. And he had to get in there quickly; he feared for Max's safety. There was a way in, obviously, for National Park's personnel made the trip on a regular basis, but he didn't have time to find and navigate it. He had to locate, if at all possible, a spot to land the plane in the valley itself. He moved the plane out over the valley, riding the winds that encircled this fortress built by nature.

The forest growth in the valley below was thick indeed. Landing here would be impossible. But in the distance, The Wraith could make out a thinning of the foliage, a solid green mass that he felt sure was an open field.

A landing place, perhaps?

He had to find out; he pressed the Northrup on toward it.

Suddenly, a mighty explosion ripped through the plane's right wing, blowing it clean off in a fiery inferno. The plane banked, unable to remain airborne, and began to zigzag down toward the forest below.

~ Chapter 6 ~

The Wraith clutched the stick, tried his best to gear the plane back under control, but to no avail. The stick shook violently in his hands. His muscles strained with the effort to maintain control. Without both wings intact, the Northrup had no way of remaining in the air, and he soon realized that if he didn't land soon, crashing was inevitable. Moving as fast as he could, he prepared to eject himself from the plunging plane. Scrambling, he managed to free himself from his harness and, an instant later, he was out, freefalling toward the earth.

Descending at an incredible speed, he grabbed hold of each end of his silken cloak, and let the air take hold of it as though it were a parachute. The Wraith silently praised Max's ingenuity in his fight against evil, including the sturdier, new cape Max had recently introduced. While it felt and appeared silken in nature, it was made of a material—its properties

known only to Max, though the Irishman did reveal its
design was based somewhat on the skin of the Australian
sugar glider—strong enough to be used as a parachute under
extraordinary conditions where a regulation chute would
prove useless. Gliding downward, his mind returned to the
subject of rescuing Max, his determination growing to not
only survive, but find those responsible and punish them.

The wind battered him harshly, but his cloak held firm,
and his descent, while hardly comfortable, was as safe and
assured as could be hoped for. The deafening sound of the
Northrup crashing into a cliff face nearby jolted him to pay
attention to the ever-nearing tree line, and the ground located
somewhere underneath.

He landed hard, somehow managing to knife through a
small gap in the tree line. After a moment to catch his breath
and thank the fates, he pulled himself up slowly, and found
he was shaken though uninjured. Although he had no way of
knowing where Max was being held, he knew his friend was
almost surely a long way from where he was, and getting
there wouldn't be easy. First things first: he had to inspect the
wreckage of the plane, to find out what had happened in the
air and perhaps get an idea of what he was dealing with. He
quickly got his bearings, and trudged off through the lush,
dense foliage.

The going was treacherous. He had landed in an elevated
part of the valley, up in the forested hills, and the scrub here
was extremely thick. However, his body conditioned for the
most vigorous exercise, he soon reached the destroyed
Northrup. Portions of the wreckage were engorged in flame,
but The Wraith didn't need to get too close to determine the
cause of the explosion. He could clearly see the signs of a
missile hit—he'd trained years ago with a retired general he'd
befriended to learn to recognize all kinds of weaponry and

incendiary blasts—and the evidence of such a hit was there before him.

A guided missile, he thought, *that's some serious firepower. They obviously don't want anyone coming too close...but how are the National Park's officers able to access this area without hindrance? Unless the villains are so well hidden and far enough away from the site of the Espinosa Pine trees to be safe from detection. Which would mean, I was expected—This was a trap!*

* * * * * *

Sloan and Perez were crammed into the small office of Howard Boynce at the City Morgue, co-coordinating the search of the victims' belongings, places of residence, employment, and history of movement for the last week or two. Everyone involved realized what a mammoth task such a search was, but they also knew the potential for more deaths lingered if they didn't succeed. That thought spurred them to ever-heightened acts of determination.

Hours passed, calls were made and received, but nothing in common—in enough numbers to be viable—was found. Sloan, never the most patient man at the best of times, soon showed his frustration by slamming his fist on the table, startling both Perez and Boynce. "Dammit! This sitting here and waiting is killing me."

"This is a big job. You know it's going to take time. Your officers are out there doing the hard yards," Boynce said.

"I know, I know, but it doesn't make the waiting any easier. Besides, I still hoped for a miracle."

At that, the phone rang, and Sloan pounced on it, answering on the first ring. "Sloan here," he said eagerly. "They what? Okay, that's a start, but keep checking. We need to know if that's spread out over all the victims' homes. Bring a sample back to the morgue ASAP."

"A break?" Perez asked after he laid the phone back on its cradle.

"Could be. Cops have found a specific brand of yogurt in many of the victims' homes. This is obviously not conclusive, but it's the first possible link we've found. We have a sample coming in, so we'll know soon enough if we have a winner."

Boynce stood and headed toward the door. "We have to get the lab prepared for intensive analysis. If this yogurt is the agent, we'll find out as quickly as possible.

* * * * * *

The city streets were still deserted as night began to fall. Everyone wanted to remain in the relative safety of their homes. While The Wraith was busy dealing with the disappearance of Max, and the police handling the virus situation, Leena thought it best to continue The Wraith's patrols of the city on her own. There was no question of staying at home and waiting things out—she wasn't that kind of girl. And so she hit the streets, for she knew that despite the virtual calm, crime never rested in Metro City.

Outfitted in the skin-tight black outfit she usually wore when she accompanied The Wraith on a mission, she sat on her haunches on the ledge of an old-style building, ornately decorated with sculptures and perching gargoyles. Leena surveyed her surroundings, watching, listening, like a belligerent hawk eying its next victim. She tried as much as possible to push other matters from her mind—the safety of Paul and Max, the stopping of this plague. She knew she needed to focus on the job at hand.

Peering down to the alley below, she spotted two sinister-looking individuals, one of which was brandishing a baseball bat. She couldn't make out if the second was holding anything. She decided to keep a watchful eye on the two, following their course through the alley and beyond.

* * * * * *

The two armed youths–for neither was any older than twenty–entered Gardenie's City Deli, one of the few stores left open in this part of the city, and a prime target for anyone with malice on their minds. Only one person was on staff in the deli, an overweight, elderly Italian man–whom those who lived in the neighborhood knew as Mr. Gardenie himself–and he greeted the two with a smile and a hearty hello. Then he saw their weapons.

"Hey! What you doing in my shop?" cried Mr. Gardenie.

"Give us your cash, fatty!" demanded the first youth, a tall skinny boy with pockmarked skin, wielding a flick-knife. The second, a shorter, calmer looking young man, appeared behind the other.

"Nick, I don't know about this," he said. He held the baseball bat semi-aloft.

"Idiot! Don't use my name!" Nick snapped back. He turned back toward Mr. Gardenie, who hadn't moved from his spot behind the cluttered counter. "I said give us all your cash!"

The nervous youth, at the sound of footsteps behind him, swiveled to find a young woman–clad in a body-hugging black lycra suit–entering the Deli. The expression on her face was a mixture of fear and incredulity. "Hey, Nick," he cried.

Nick turned his head, while keeping his knife pointed at the hapless Deli owner. "You!" he yelled at the woman. "Get over here!"

She looked at the two youths, appearing nervous and frightened. "I...I won't cause any trouble."

Nick smiled and moved over to her, flashing his knife. "She looks nice and soft," he said.

She began to shake with apparent fright, which only egged Nick on even more.

"You wanna party, baby?"

"Nick, we don't have time for this," his partner muttered.

"Shuddup!" Nick barked. "And you" —he pointed his knife at Mr. Gardenie— "get that cash over here. Now!"

"You leave her alone," Mr. Gardenie said, finally removing the cash from his register then shuffling around the counter.

"Is that it?" Nick asked, seeing the flimsy takings in Mr. Gardenie's hand. "I need more!"

At this, the woman sprung into action, like a panther, fast and lupine. She grabbed Nick's arm good and tight, and brought her knee up into it, breaking his arm at the elbow. Nick screamed.

"You bit—" he started to yelp.

The woman smashed her fist into his face, sending him to the floor, where he lay whimpering. He looked up through bleary eyes.

Mr. Gardenie approached her, his expression a mixture of shock and admiration. "Miss, I cannot thank you enough."

The young woman appeared in a hurry though. The other punk had made a hasty retreat from the deli, and she appeared eager to get out of there. "I'm sorry to rush off like this, but I'm sure you understand. Call the police. They'll come and pick up this guy." She then handcuffed the injured Nick and sprinted from the establishment.

* * * * * *

Outside, the streets were empty save for one person standing across the street from the deli. Leena looked either way, trying to see if she could still spot the fleeing punk, but couldn't. The stranger across from her pointed down the street to her left, indicating the youth's path. Leena waved her thanks, and ran in that direction.

As she ran, her thoughts returned to Paul's search for Max, the police's frantic quest to halt the spread of the virus, and the survival of the city. She realized again the perils of her life and of her life's mission. To be a part of Paul's life, to be with him, she had to make drastic changes to her own life, changes that most people would have been unwilling to make. She, however, knew it had been worth it. To be with the man she loved more than life itself, to share in his joy, his pain, his glory—mixed with the triumphs and defeats of her own—surely a goal worthy of any woman.

She spotted her quarry in the distance. The guy was slow, his footfalls unsure and uneven.

Drunk, perhaps?

She would catch up to him easily. He suddenly vanished from sight, having ducked into an adjacent alley. Leena quickened her pace, not wanting to allow him to get away with his meager takings.

* * * * * *

The young man sputtered and coughed as he retreated deep into an alley strewn with rubbish, debris and an open, running sewer. He stopped and leaned against the wall nearest him, seeing and smelling the bodies of two bums lying dead nearby, causing him to breathe heavily and cough still more.

"I-I'm free..." he breathed.

He looked around. The alley was deserted save for the corpses; everything was still. He smiled, snickered softly to himself, and rested a moment longer, attempting to get his breath back despite the stench of death aggravating his senses.

At that moment, the silence and peace of the moment was shattered by a whizzing sound. Before he could even wonder at the noise, he was pressed tightly against the wall, immobilized, unable to break free.

"Hey!" he cried, panicking. He was able to get a slight view of his predicament, though he was only barely able to move his head. He had been caught in an intricate, and extremely strong, net-like material, which had him pinned from head to toe. Gleaming silver pins secured the net—and him—to the wall.

"What the hell?" he shrieked.

"Tsk, tsk" the young woman from the deli said, emerging from the gloom of the shadows, then drawing near. "I prefer my thugs to be a little better mannered."

The youth continued struggling, but it achieved nothing. "Who...who are you?" he said.

She pressed in close, an expression of menace on her face. "Who I am is of no concern to you. You need to start thinking of what's going to happen to you, and perhaps contemplate your future."

"Wha...wha..." he stuttered. He blinked. And the woman was gone.

* * * * * *

The Wraith turned and looked up the steep slope of the adjacent hillside. He was at the outer edge of the valley, and while he was already in an elevated position, the forest of alder bushes and birches was still too thick to be able to obtain any proper bearings. Through the trees in the opposite direction, he noticed a bare outcropping of rock, and thought it possible to be able to gain a better view of the valley from there.

Scrambling up, the thickets and brambles snagged at his uniform. He crested the hill, and was able to peer out over the forest below. The narrow but lengthy valley stretched out before him. What appeared to be a small lake—or perhaps a river—sat near the valley's center.

Hmm, he thought. *I am at the outer edge of the valley.* He removed a pair of mini-binoculars from his belt. *I'm quite high up. It'll take a bit of walking just to reach the bottom. And then which direction?*

Questions beat in his brain like a hammer. He quickly determined to reach the bottom of the valley first then decide his next move from there.

Moving back down the steep slope through the thick undergrowth was slow going. The Wraith worried about Max's safety. Obviously Max had been taken and used as a lure to get him out there.

But why? And who was responsible?

He wondered if, by chance, those responsible were also the instigators of the plague emergency currently sweeping through the city.

The plague!

During his tribulations, he'd briefly forgotten about it. As he continued the arduous trek downward, he yearned to see his beloved Leena again and hoped she was able to cope in the city alone. Hoped above all that she and the police force had determined the source of the plague. He smiled. He had trained her well, and suspected she was out patrolling the city's streets at that very moment. As to the authorities...all he could do was trust in Leena's ability to help them.

* * * * * *

The scene in the City Morgue was as horrific—and chaotic—as ever. Perez sat inside Howard Boynce's office, peering out the open door toward her partner, who was in the main workroom, pacing impatiently amongst the rows of corpses.

"Bob, you're driving me crazy," Perez said.

Before he could reply, Boynce appeared from an adjacent lab, the smile on his face indicating the breakthrough they had been hoping—praying—for had been reached.

"You're smiling, Howard," Sloan said.

"The yogurt sample that was brought in yielded positive results," Boynce revealed. "It's laced with the pseudo-virus."

"That's great," Sloan said. "Then we can put a stop to this."

"Yes and no," Boynce said, as Perez joined them. "I still have no idea what on Earth this is, and have no way of developing a cure, certainly not in quick time, and most likely never with the equipment we have here. We'll pass this along to the Feds as soon as we can get the quarantine lifted. But now that we know the source of the plague, we can control it, and that should hopefully stop the slaughter."

Perez looked sharply at the two men. "It's not a widely known brand, which is why more people weren't killed. We could have potentially lost millions had this stuff been placed in Corn Flakes or Spam, say." Her partner shivered. "We have to make sure this yogurt wasn't the only source."

"We're testing various products as they come in, just to make sure. So far, all negative. Looks like it was the yogurt alone," said Boynce.

"But why?" Sloan asked. "This seems too sophisticated for a terrorist attack. They like to make an instant impact with bombs or suicide attacks. This is different." He started to pace again as he spoke. "There's menace behind this, there's purpose. We just have to find out what that is."

"And above all," added Perez, "enable a complete recall of Snowy's Yogurt. We need to get every sample of it off store shelves, and let people know to throw any unopened tubs into the trash. That means getting the word out through all media outlets."

Sloan grabbed his jacket, which he'd hung on sheet-covered feet of a nearby cadaver, and raced for the exit. "Let's go, Perez, we have work to do."

* * * * * *

As The Wraith neared the bottom of the hill, the underbrush thinned, grass replacing bramble, the thin silver birches allowing more sunlight to break through. Despite the precarious journey, he'd made good time, adopting the half-trot, half-lope that the woods-runners of the long-gone local Indians had used in the area many years before.

Soon, having reached the valley's bottom, he arrived at a path, what appeared to be a game trail. His way was assured to be smoother, at least for the time being. His pace quickened. The trail was leading toward the center of the valley, or so it seemed. He followed the path.

The game trail stopped at a small brook. He bent down, sampling the cool, refreshing water, and quenched his thirst. The day was warming up, what breeze there was now choked off by the trees. He still had no idea of exactly which direction to take, but he knew he had to get there as quickly as possible. He stood again and turned, trying to determine his next course of action. The Wraith hoped he wouldn't be too late to save the gallant man who had thrown in his lot with the original Sanderson all those years ago. The thought suddenly occurred to him—there was no guarantee Max was still alive. Alive or dead, Max's only purpose to those responsible was to lure The Wraith there, and they had succeeded. As the thought worked maddeningly in his head, The Wraith labored onwards, jogging adjacent to the brook for as long as possible.

For what seemed an eternity, he followed the brook, constantly glancing side-to-side for any sign of life. The imposing cliff faces of the surrounding mountains loomed on either side of him, and the dense forest encroaching the plain he currently strode upon seemed to cry out with hidden menace. He continued along the path, grateful for the flattened grassy surface.

The brook soon narrowed into a small, marshy spring. Ordinarily, the scene would be that of pristine beauty, of nature unspoiled by the hand of man, but The Wraith somehow found his surroundings etched with mystery, an eeriness he couldn't describe or calculate, but nevertheless an underlying sense of that felt very real to him. He again looked to either side, but saw nothing but trees and the impressive proportions of the surrounding cliffs. The plain came to an abrupt end, the forest of maples, birches and pines intruding on the now marshy path.

As The Wraith entered the forest, he heard a sharp crack, quickly recognizing the sound of a branch snapping. He ducked promptly behind the nearest cover—a particularly wide oak tree—and waited, holding his breath. He heard another branch snap. And another. A whistle rose up and was drawing near. Closer. And closer. Soon, the whistle was almost upon him. Keeping surprise on his side, he leapt out, crash tackled the source of the whistle, and pinned the young man to the ground, pressing his right forearm into the man's throat.

"Ack…" was all the young man could manage to say. He was of average height, with sandy hair and a youthful complexion. The Wraith estimated he was no older than twenty.

"Talk!" The Wraith growled, and he slackened his grip slightly. But only slightly.

The young man coughed before replying. "You're The—The—"

The Wraith yanked him to his feet. "Who are you, what are you doing here?"

"My name's Adam. I live here," he said. He tried to regain some measure of composure.

The Wraith scoffed. "You can't have been here more than a week, judging by your appearance. What are you doing here?"

"I told you," Adam replied, "I live here. You're right: I've only been here just over a week. I tired of the world's obsession with technology, of polluting the environment, of harming his fellow man. I wanted to see if I could make it on my own, in the wilderness, like Theroux."

The Wraith eyed him with suspicion. He wondered how likely it would be to come across another human being in such a remote, hidden place as this without the person being involved in Max's kidnapping. But the look on Adam's face, the innocence he exhibited, presently convinced him of the truth of his words.

"You're in potential danger here," The Wraith said.

"Danger? I've seen no signs of any danger."

Almost right after he said that, The Wraith's acute sense of hearing picked up the distant and very soft sound of something whizzing through the air. Before either he or Adam could react, a small dart plunged into each of them—one in The Wraith's neck, the other into Adam's arm. The effect was swift.

Darkness.

~ Chapter 7 ~

Late afternoon the next day, the Metro City Police headquarters was buzzing with activity. Now that the truth had been discovered about the virus and where it had come from, the staff had returned in full—minus those who had died—feeling more confident that the end of this horror was finally in sight.

Seated at his desk, Sloan was talking on the phone as his partner approached him, a smile on her face.

"We're making progress," Perez said. "We've nearly cleared all the stores of Snowy's Yogurt, and the media outlets have been broadcasting all day, warning the public."

"Hallelujah," Sloan said, breathing a little easier. He concluded his call and set the phone on its cradle.

"And the Feds are now helping clearing the bodies throughout the city. And, best of all, no more fatalities have been reported."

"Any word on the *amount* of casualties?" Commissioner Harrison asked, having joined the pair at Sloan's desk.

"Still only estimates, Commissioner," Perez answered. "So far, the figure stands at at least five thousand, but it could easily be more. We should have a better estimate soon."

The three officers stared at each other in sullen silence at the reality of Perez's words. So many people lost.

"Snowy's Yogurt... Do we have men down at the factory?" Harrison asked.

"Yeah, there now," Sloan replied. "Perez and I were just heading out there."

"Good," Harrison said. "We need to know how that filth got into those tubs and who was responsible." He paused briefly. "I agree, though, that this is clearly not the work of external terrorists. But we can't yet discount an internal terrorism theory."

"Could just be some disgruntled employee," Sloan added.

"Could be, though I doubt it. Still, we need to cover all the bases," Harrison said.

"Okay, Perez. Let's get going. Snowy's is on the other side of town, and we need to have a few words with their company executives."

* * * * * *

Latham brooded alone in his study at home. As with most other people in the city, he'd been forced to remain at home during the recent crisis, and had spent the time working furiously to rescue the reputation of the city—and his business—in that time. While money always talked, especially in his business dealings, his overseas contacts had become worried. Metro City wasn't the safest place to conduct business anymore. First, The Wraith had become a major problem. Then, large portions of the city had been destroyed through the vengeance of the Cobra, followed in quick succession by the invasion of Ma Tzi into Latham's stronghold—and now the plague. Latham grunted in frustration, laid his pen down, and rubbed his eyes.

"Damn..." he whispered to himself.

A moment later, Charlie Grieco entered with his usual confident swagger.

"Where have you been?" Latham demanded.

Grieco slowly took the chair in front of the desk, his lascivious smile never leaving his face.

"Business, Mr. Latham, strengthening our core base," he said.

Latham stood, frustrated, angry and exhausted. "I didn't authorize you to make any deals. I need you here right now. I'm working to save this empire, and you're off playing patty cake somewhere."

"Mr. Latham, trust me, everything is under control."

This wasn't the time to push him. "Under control? I'm barely holding the threads of my business together and you're telling me everything is under control?" He came beside Grieco.

"Mr. Latham, I'm telling you, I've been looking after your best interests. You're just going to have to trust me on this," he said.

Latham stared at him a few moments then started to pace back and forth alongside his desk. "I've had about enough of your disobedience," he said. He stared at his deputy. "Get outta here, Charlie. I'll deal with you later."

Grieco stood, but didn't move any further. His smile had finally vanished. "One day, there's gonna be a reckoning, old man!" And he left the study before Latham could react.

* * * * * *

"Switch it off," Tzi ordered. He was seated in front of his repaired console, surrounded by his men, who worked at their stations. The man nearest him immediately acquiesced, flicking a switch on the console as per his master's orders.

"The antagonism grows between Mr. Latham and our newfound ally. Good," said Tzi. "I think we can use this situation to our advantage." He stood and began to stroll slowly back to his throne. "Yes, I foresee an excellent result from this arrangement. Excellent for me, that is, but perhaps not so good an outcome for Mr. Latham...or his deputy."

He sat down and ruminated over his words, allowing himself the luxury of a small, subtle smile.

* * * * * *

The Wraith came to and found himself surrounded by darkness, unable to see a thing. He was lying on a hard surface, but that was all he could tell. His mind was still foggy, his thoughts muddled, and the memory of what led him there eluded him. He heard a soft, rustling sound. He raised his body upward slightly; his head throbbed with an extreme headache.

"Who's there?" he managed to utter.

"Chief?" a familiar voice replied weakly.

"M-Max..." The name caught in The Wraith's throat. His mouth was parched, but he was slowly regaining his composure. "Max, are you okay?"

"I think so," Max replied. "I don't feel any pain. The Daimler protected me from the brunt of the crash."

"Where are we? Can you tell me anything about where we are and who we're being held by?"

"It's the Cobra's men, possibly the Cobra himself. I followed Magnus Khan and his entourage from the city and...I fell for their trap hook, line and sinker."

The Wraith could hear frustration and anger in Max's voice. This had all been a well-orchestrated trap, first with Max and now himself, the latter which the Dread Avenger had anticipated, but was forcibly entered into, for the sake of Max's life.

"We're dealing with a very resourceful and dangerous group. They knew exactly how to take us while our attention was diverted elsewhere, focused on saving the city from the plague," The Wraith said.

"Wha-wha's happenin'?" a voice beside them said.

The Wraith remembered the young man and realized they had both been captured. "It's okay, Adam, though we seem to be imprisoned here."

"Wraith?" Adam said weakly.

The Wraith ignored him and tried to stand atop still wobbly feet. His strength, however, returned to him quickly, flooding his limbs with the vitality needed for what they had to do: escape. It was dark and silent, the kind of silence that one could almost drown in. The Wraith suddenly realized he was no longer wearing his costume. He had been stripped down to his boxers while he had been unconscious, and wondered if Max and Adam had received the same treatment.

He stretched his arms out, trying to make sense of his surroundings in the darkness. He managed to take three steps forward before feeling the icy-cold barriers of iron bars in his hands. He grabbed them, tested their strength. There was no budging them. He followed their course to his right, and quickly reached the corner. He repeated the move in the opposite direction, and reached the other corner within moments. He next followed the bars up above his head and found they stretched out overhead, completely encircling the trio.

"Well, we're in a steel cage, only a few feet across, but just enough room to stand in," The Wraith said.

"Hey!" Max cried. "I'm naked...well, almost."

"Me too," Adam said, the sound of their voices and of them standing to join The Wraith the only sound that could be heard.

"Hey, who are you?" Max asked.

"This is Adam," The Wraith said. "We met in the valley."

"A touching scene," a voice interrupted. It had been a long time since The Wraith had heard it, but once he heard a voice, it never left him, especially one as menacing as that of Magnus Khan. Instantly, a powerful overhead light streamed on, blinding him and no doubt Max and Adam as well. The Wraith shielded his eyes, allowing them the extra few seconds of adjustment they needed to see his quarry. Magnus Khan strode toward the cage, a smug expression upon his face.

"I hope you are enjoying your quarters." Khan sneered.

They were in a large, cavernous, square-shaped room, bereft of any furnishings, of any distinguishing characteristics or markings.

"Khan!" The Wraith growled.

Khan edged closer to the bars, but refrained from coming too close to be in any danger. "Round three is mine, Wraith. And there will not be a round four."

The Wraith seethed with anger. Khan was the Cobra's chief emissary, and personally responsible for the untold deaths of hundreds, if not thousands, of elderly homeless men as part of the Cobra's master plan to create an army of the homeless. Those considered too old or frail were dealt with mercilessly as a way of goading The Wraith that such an atrocity could occur in his city. The rest had been kidnapped, brainwashed, indoctrinated, and became a true army from hell!

"So the Cobra *is* alive," The Wraith said. "Where is Abdelkrim?"

Khan laughed. "The Mistress said you would react in such a way. How predictable you are. You were led here like a parent guiding its child."

"Mistress?" Max queried.

"Yes," a female voice rang out. A captivating woman, outfitted in a tight, form-fitting black outfit with a plunging neckline, appeared from behind Magnus Khan. Her long, flowing hair fell forward over her shoulders, giving her an almost Lady Godiva-like appearance. She was joined by several, burly ninjas, obviously her bodyguards. The Wraith clenched his jaw.

"Who are you? Are you responsible for the plague?" The Wraith demanded.

The woman slinked toward the cage, sashaying her hips seductively. "Aren't you full of questions," she said. "To your latter question, yes, but I'm sure you hardly needed to ask me that. As for who I am, I am Natalya Blackova, successor to the great Cobra. I will conquer in his stead, in his name," she said with complete, straightforward sincerity. "And you are here to satisfy my vengeance, for you are responsible for his demise." Those last words oozed with venomous promise. The Wraith could clearly see that behind that veil of beauty was an evil of incalculable depth.

The Wraith mocked his captors. "Your plan has failed. Your agent for the distribution of the virus has been discovered. The city has been saved. And I promise you'll pay for the deaths of thousands of innocents."

The woman took a step back, a look of displeasure on her attractive features. "Come, come, did you think I would not anticipate your intervention? Did you not think I had other avenues for distribution? Do you take me for a fool?"

While her accent gave away her nationality, her appearance was exotic enough to suggest a mixed lineage. The Wraith also recognized her as the pilot of the airship which had been the Cobra's attempt at escape during their last encounter. And, oddly, he felt himself strangely drawn to her despite the intense anger and hatred welling inside him for her despicable actions. He tried to shake the feeling. He turned to Max, who was now beside him, his face pressed up against the bars, staring deeply at Blackova as she took a few steps back from the cage. The Wraith turned in the opposite direction and noted the same reaction in Adam. Puzzled, The Wraith attempted to turn his mind back to his anger, which despite the curious mix of emotions flooding him, hadn't subsided.

"I mustn't tarry," Blackova said as she turned on her heels. "I have a city to destroy and a people to conquer. Your role in my master plan will be revealed to you in due course." She had arrived at the room's only exit. "I shall return shortly." And with that, she left, her bodyguards and Khan followed closely behind.

* * * * * *

As Sloan and Perez slowed their unmarked down, rounding a corner, the Snowy's Yogurt factory emerged through the windshield. The factory's distinctive snowman logo spun gently atop the building's roof.

"Who would have ever thought such a friendly face would be responsible for such horror," Perez said, pointing to the Snowy statue. Sloan huffed, but said nothing, and parked the car as close to the factory's front entrance as possible.

The two detectives hurried to find the Chief Executive's office, and found two officers there accompanying Harold Waldheim, who was waiting to be questioned.

"Mr. Waldheim, thank you very much for agreeing to this interview," Sloan said.

"Not at all," Waldheim replied, clearly exasperated with all this attention. He was a middle-aged man of slightly less-than-average height, and an unruly mop of noticeably dyed beige hair. "I can't tell you how horrified I am that our product has been used for such purposes. I hope you can get to the bottom of all this."

"That's what we're here for," Sloan said.

"Now, Mr. Waldheim, we need a complete inventory of your staff, including any background material you may have," Perez said. "And if you have any information yourself, now's the time to tell us."

One of the police officers handed Sloan a folder. "Here's the staff information we thought you'd want ASAP."

"And I have nothing to add myself," Waldheim quickly said. "I have no knowledge of how our product was infused with that poison or who was responsible."

Perez turned to face her partner. "We don't know it was even done here. In fact, I doubt it. The safeguards would be too restrictive."

"Not for the Chief Executive," Sloan said.

"Now wait just a minute!" Waldheim said, raising his voice. "That sounds like an accusation, and one without merit or evidence." He stood, trying to appear tall. "I think I should wait for my lawyer before saying anything else."

Sloan looked to Perez. He knew that stance and his suspicions were immediately raised by Waldheim's defiance and quick change in attitude. His plan had worked and he was confident in his own powers of persuasion to get a confession—or at the very least, further clues–before any intervention by some cashed up shark of the law.

"Take a seat please, Mr. Waldheim, and I'm sure we can come to some sort of an arrangement," Sloan said, trying to calm him.

Before Waldheim or anyone else could reply, a shot rang out, shattering the office window and sending Waldheim to the floor in a split-second.

"Jeez, an assassination!" Sloan yelled as everyone hit the floor. "Check Waldheim, Perez."

Perez crawled over to Waldheim's body. "Perfect shot to the head; he never had a chance."

"We have our answer then: it was Waldheim who poisoned the yogurt. But why? Money?" Sloan said, still hugging the floor.

Perez inched over to the open window, and carefully peered out. "No sign of the assassin, Bob."

"Call it in," Sloan said to the officer nearest him. "And get some backup here, in case the assassin is still out there."

Perez got to her feet and dusted herself off. "Whoever it was must be long gone. The job's done; they're not gonna stick around to get caught."

Everyone else stood. Sloan repeated to the officer, "Call it in now!" The officer grabbed his radio, and he and his partner swiftly exited the office. Sloan crouched alongside Waldheim's body and examined the wound carefully. It wasn't pretty; a large amount of blood was pooling on the floor by the body's head, and there was a substantial red splatter on the wall from the impact of the bullet.

"It was a high-powered shot, a rifle from the sound of it, but we need C.S.I. down here pronto," Sloan declared. "The bullet's there in the wall." He pointed at the stain.

Perez moved over beside him and asked, "What's going on here? Even with Waldheim's murder, we've already discovered the source of the virus; we've discovered the one responsible for placing it in the yogurt. So why was Waldheim silenced?"

"Obviously to prevent us from learning the true identity of those responsible, the person or group behind Waldheim. This is more than just terrorism, Perez. This is something much more."

* * * * * *

The cavernous room where The Wraith and his comrades were imprisoned was once again plunged into pitch darkness.

"This is hopeless," Adam said.

"There's always hope," Max replied.

"I wish they'd left me my cowl," The Wraith said. "I could have examined the cage for any potential areas to exploit an escape. What I saw of the room indicates only one exit, though my attention was somewhat lacking, I admit."

"Now that you mention it..." Max breathed. "I did find that lady rather captivating..." He stopped himself short. "What am I saying?"

"I felt the same thing," Adam said.

"Somehow," The Wraith continued, "this Natalya Blackova has some abilities to beguile men. Perhaps an offshoot of the mesmerizing ability the Cobra exhibited?"

"That's right. The Cobra did have such a power," Max said. "It could, I guess, have been transferred, partially or otherwise, to this woman."

"Perhaps, but it feels different somehow, Max," The Wraith said. "But I'm certain the Cobra was somehow responsible for her powers. However, that isn't our first priority. We need to get out of this cage and then find—"

The overhead lights snapped on again. Magnus Khan quickly appeared at the door.

"Your presence is required in the throne room," Khan boomed.

"Throne room?" Max said. "What for?"

"It is time for you to acquit yourselves in the arena—as gladiators!"

~ Chapter 8 ~

Khan and a group of his ninjas led The Wraith, Max and Adam into the throne room, an even larger room than where they had been imprisoned, and far more impressive. The Wraith estimated the room to perhaps be fifty feet long and wide and nearly twenty feet high. The ceiling was covered with remarkable sculptured patterns, entirely abstract, but suggestive of a mix of cultures and mythologies; Greek and Egyptian being the two most recognizable to The Wraith.

Lining three of the four walls was a mass of ninjas, in columns five thick, and chanting in unison in a language the Dread Avenger did not recognize. At the head of this architecturally ornate room, seated on a throne appearing to be made out of human skulls, was Natalya Blackova. Wearing a revealing outfit, she smiled sensually at them as they walking into the center of the room, which was shaped and positioned almost like the floor of a gymnastic sports stadium, with the audience gathered around the outside fringe.

"Welcome, Wraith. I have decided a suitable fate for you and your men. To battle here, for my enjoyment, in the arena —for your lives!"

The chanting from the horde of ninjas increased tempo; it irritated The Wraith. He remained silent, his muscled body rigid and tense, ready for action.

"Nothing to say?" Blackova asked. "Perhaps it is for the best." She stood, and cavorted down the three steps from her throne, toward the three men. "You'll be battling amongst yourselves for the privilege to be slaughtered by my own hands. An honor the victor will no doubt fail to appreciate." She moved in close to The Wraith, her nose touching his chin. She ran her index finger along the contours of his clenched jaw.

"We won't...fight..." The Wraith found himself struggling to say. Blackova's influence was beginning to affect him.

Blackova ignored him and moved on to Max, pressing her body–and her ample bosom–against his naked chest. She whispered something into his ear before moving over to Adam and giving him a soft, but sultry, kiss on the cheek. After that, she returned to face the Dread Avenger.

"Oh, I think you will," she said. "I have a certain...influence...with men, as I am sure you have not failed to notice." She slowly circled The Wraith, who, despite his intense fury, could not take his eyes off her. "Do you not desire me? Am I not everything you have ever wanted?"

Her voice echoed in his head. He tried to shake the feeling, but he couldn't help recognizing she had the most beautiful, captivating voice he'd ever heard.

No! he thought.

Blackova retreated to her throne, briefly turning to smile at the three, who were now completely under her spell. Lifting her flowing gown elegantly, revealing slim, well-shaped thighs, she sat back down.

"Here is your cowl," she said, pointing at Khan, who produced the mask and handed it to The Wraith. "I know you prefer to be properly outfitted for battle. You will forgive me if I don't return the rest of your suit and belt to you. I am well aware of the danger both pose to me."

The Wraith stirred at this statement, an idea striking him, but he remained still and silent. After a pause, he donned his cowl. "I am ready," he said.

Blackova smiled, obviously delighted at the success of overpowering the three men. "You are, naturally, the superior of the others, so I thought it best that you do battle with the both of them. Prepare them!"

Khan stepped forward, positioned Max and Adam—both still clearly and completely bewitched by the charm's of the evil seductress—at one end of the mat, The Wraith at the other.

"Fight for me, my darlings—to the death!" Blackova said.

Rage etched on their faces, Max and Adam stepped forward, fully intent to render The Wraith limb-from-limb. The Wraith, while affected somewhat by Blackova's power, was nevertheless still in control, and he had an idea, but all depended on how the impending battle progressed.

Max and Adam lunged forward, their anger driving them to attack. The Wraith sidestepped their assault and spun round, readying himself. Max and Adam were no longer themselves, willing to do anything Natalya Blackova bade them, even against their will. As Max and Adam prepared to attack again, The Wraith bandied strategies around in his mind. He knew he was capable of taking both with relative ease, but their safety was of paramount importance to him. He decided Adam—presumably the less skilled—needed to be dealt with first, to take him out of the equation.

Max approached first. The Wraith performed a swift, precise leg sweep, taking Max's legs out from under him, sending his friend tumbling to the floor. For a brief moment, Adam was isolated and The Wraith took immediate action, grabbing him at the base of the throat, and before Adam could react, squeezed. Adam instantly ceased struggling, and fell in a heap to the floor, unconscious. With the young man out of the way, The Wraith could concentrate on dealing with Max.

Max, his fury visibly growing, stepped up his attack. Trained by The Wraith, Max was a proficient combatant, skilled in a variety of hand-to-hand combat disciplines, but that was tempered by his age, his physical condition, and his mental state (which was currently clouded by Blackova's charms).

Max let loose with a violent swing; The Wraith ducked. The Irishman swung again; The Wraith avoided the blow. Max may not have been at his best, but the Dread Avenger knew he would see stars if one of those blows connected. Max grunted and charged him, grabbing The Wraith in a bear hug. The Wraith grimaced, groaning in pain, as Max squeezed tighter and tighter.

"Max...think of what you're doing?" The Wraith said through clenched teeth. He looked straight into his comrade's eyes; Max's eyes were glazed over, without recognition that he was fighting his friend. "Fight her, Max. Fight her!"

Max snarled like a caged animal, his grip growing ever tighter. The intense chanting of the amassed crowd droned in The Wraith's skull like a jackhammer.

Blackova said something. The Wraith couldn't make out her words, and he doubted Max did either, not in his current state. Max continued to squeeze, showing incredible strength, undoubtedly fueled by adrenalin and his ignited passion to fight for a woman whom controlled his mind. With unconsciousness looming, The Wraith lashed out as best he could, slamming his right heel into the toes of Max's left foot. Max yelped—not so much in pain, for the blow was weak—but evident surprise, surprise enough for his grip to loosen. The Wraith, with some effort, managed to wriggle free.

It was clear now that he needed to not only deal with Max, but cure him of this evil influence. With Max's next onslaught, which was quick in coming, The Wraith managed to secure the Irishman's arm, twisting it behind Max's back, causing Max considerable pain. The Wraith twisted and turned, ultimately forcing Max to his knees. Having gained an advantage, he spun Max around and unleashed his Judgment Stare on him.

"Forgive me, but this is for your own good," The Wraith said as the Eyes of Judgment crackled and shimmered with intense, supernatural energy.

Max screamed.

"What is this?" screamed Blackova, who shot to her feet. "How can this be? You are without your costume!" Her distress affected the entire room, the chanting instantly ceasing, replaced by murmurs of confusion and chaos.

The Wraith ended the Judgment Stare, utilizing his ability just long enough to break the hold Blackova had over Max, and ensuring she could never again captivate him as she had. Sweat streamed from Max's brow, but he was conscious, and he was recovered. Blackova had obviously thought his power emanated from his suit, not from within as it truly did.

"Ch-Chief?" Max stammered.

The Dread Avenger reached up, carefully and efficiently lifting the knot—or what was shaped to appear as a knot—at the back of his cowl, and removed from the hollow recess within the faux knot what appeared to be several mini pain-relief capsules. His enemies obviously took his cowl at face value, without carefully examining it. While it looked for all the world very much like a bandanna with holes cut out for the eyes, it was really a complex mix of leather covering a robust resin undershell, offering him maximum comfort and protection. And it enabled Max to outfit the cowl with several unique features. The knot at the back was purely for decorative purposes—and as a precautionary measure, it housed a variety of pellets—gas, explosive, healing agents.

"Max, shield your eyes," The Wraith barked. Rapidly, he lobbed two of the capsules into the crowd of ninjas and quickly followed that by tossing two more into the overhead lighting. Before Blackova or Khan could react, a blinding flash erupted from all corners of the throne room and from the ceiling, sending a sharp, white light that seemed brighter than the sun. The Wraith squeezed his eyes shut and pressed his arm to his face to protect his vision. He knew Max would have done likewise. The combined screams of agony and shock deafened The Wraith, but it also heartened him, for he knew the desired result had been achieved.

"Chief! Blackova and Khan have escaped!" Max cried out once the flash of light had subsided.

Noting the disappearance of the two, The Wraith moved to reply, but his attention was diverted by four of the ninjas—those who had evidently averted their eyes—springing into action, ready for combat. They appeared well trained, their muscles well honed.

These are clearly no longer kidnapped homeless men, The Wraith thought.

Two of the ninjas pounced in unison, one of which executed a spinning scissor-kick aimed at The Wraith's head. The Dread Avenger managed to duck the potentially fatal blow and sprang back up, letting loose with a powerful right to the jaw of the other ninja, careening him back several feet. The first ninja resumed his attack, charging with powerful kicks and punches. The Wraith blocked and parried with equal skill, but the battle was deflecting him from his true quest, his true quarry, and he swore to himself he would make Blackova and Khan pay for their devilry.

The Eyes of Judgment again began to crackle with energy. It distracted the ninja ever-so-briefly, and The Wraith worked it to his advantage, landing a hard kick into the ninja's stomach then followed that with a kick to the head. Surprisingly, the ninja managed to avoid the brunt of the final blow and was only slightly stunned. The Wraith, his Eyes of Judgment still bristling with concentrated energy, grappled with the ninja, yanked his mask from the ninja's head, and heaved him to his feet.

"Now you will be judged!" The Wraith boomed. "Feel your very soul burn with the pain you have inflicted on others!" He maneuvered the ninja's face into the energy emanating from his chest. The ninja's scream of anguish was as sickening as it was brief, as a black-clad arm reached around The Wraith's throat, choking him.

"You will not be permitted to leave this place alive," said the third of the four ninjas that went into battle.

Struggling, The Wraith said, "I don't intend falling to the likes of you." The Wraith lashed out, his elbow plunging into the ninja's belly. The ninja appeared stunned for an instant, but his grip remained strong. The Wraith tried again, but his blow was weaker, his energy sapped, his oxygen dangerously cut off.

His mind raced. *Could I die at the hands of some...lackey? To fail at this stage, allowing the villains free reign over the city, over the country! And Leena...darling Leena...*

With unconsciousness threatening, a powerful cracking sound ended the struggle. The Wraith, now freed, dropped to his knees and took in a lungful of air. He turned to find Max standing behind him, smiling.

"I'm sorry it took me so long, Chief, but that other one wasn't easy to dispose of." He pointed to another ninja—the fourth—lying nearby on the mat, prone.

The throne room was in chaos. Both Blackova and Khan had made their escape, but the throng of ninjas were bustling about, yelling, whimpering, bumping into things.

"Your flash pellets worked, Max," The Wraith said. "Will the damage be permanent?"

"It shouldn't, but remember, I haven't been able to fully test them yet. It's possible, for some, that their blindness could be permanent!"

There was no time for remorse. Those responsible for the slaughter of thousands had escaped, and The Wraith knew he had to take up the chase or all might still be lost.

As Adam began to stir, The Wraith said, "Get him up. We need to be moving."

Max got the young man to his feet.

The Wraith moved quickly toward the curtained wall directly behind the hideous throne. Max and Adam followed closely behind.

"Hidden access way," said Max after The Wraith parted the curtains. "They ducked in here?"

"They must have. They didn't come past us through the main door."

The trio barged through the small door, coming into a darkened antechamber which was small but decorated with a variety of ornate statues of faint Asian and African origin. The Wraith pressed a point at his temple and night-vision lenses slid into place over his eyes. He scanned the room.

"There are our clothes," The Wraith said, catching sight of them. "And another door. Quickly, get dressed. We can't let them get too much of a head start on us."

Rushing from the antechamber, now fully dressed, the three ran down the barren, concrete-walled corridor, hoping to quickly find the building's exit. The corridor was a long one and twisted and turned, leading into even more corridors.

"We're in a damn maze," Max complained, the three continuing their headlong rush to find the exit. As the corridors blended one into another, they finally arrived at what appeared to be the building's front entrance.

"Wait a minute," Max said, coming to a sudden halt. "We haven't come across anyone since we left the throne room. Those ninjas...were they everyone in the building?"

"Good question," The Wraith replied. "A building this size...I can't see a criminal outfit this well organized having this few personnel. Where is everyone?"

The Wraith examined the closed double door. The door itself looked thick and strong, similar in size and shape to the entrance to a bank vault. However, there were no door handles, no apparent method of opening. There was a small, square-shaped panel by the side of the door. He pressed his hand against it. The doors slid open with a swish.

Too easy? There was no time to ponder this further.

Not knowing what more to make of this, the three went through, coming out into a small clearing at one end of the elongated valley—standing face-to-face with a battalion of ninjas!

* * * * * *

Sloan, Perez and Harrison were crowded in Harrison's cramped office, debating the current course of the investigation.

Harrison paced behind his desk, taking only two steps in each direction before being forced by the clutter to repeat the move in the other direction. "We have another body, and we're no closer to discovering those responsible for the city's plague," he said.

"Ballistics have so far turned up nothing regarding Waldheim's murder," Perez said.

"And the lab boys have also come up with zip," Sloan added.

Harrison continued pacing. "So, where does that leave us?"

Sloan rose from his chair. "We know Waldheim was behind the lacing of his own product, though whether he acted alone within the Snowy organization—we're still looking into that. As to who Waldheim was working for and why, we simply don't know yet."

"There has to be some sort of clue at Snowy's," Harrison fired back. "Something that can provide that missing link." He paused, seeming to collect his thoughts. "Get back to the factory. I can't help shake this feeling that there's something there that will tell us more."

Sloan wondered if this was the right track to take at this stage of the investigation. He and Perez had already gone over Waldheim's office with a fine-toothed comb, and other officers had searched the factory and found nothing of note. He looked at his partner and recognized her expression of doubt. Still, they'd hit a brick wall at this stage, so perhaps the commissioner was right.

"We're on it," Sloan finally said.

* * * * * *

Within the Latham Industries building, business had returned to normal. Aside from being at the head of one of the largest crime cartels on the Eastern seaboard, Robert Latham was also a very successful, legitimate businessman; Latham Industries had such varied interests as electronics, fossil fuels, casinos, the media and much more. Most workers within the building were employed within the business's legitimate enterprises; some, however, were also involved in other, more nefarious activities. One such man was Charlie Grieco...

Exiting his office, Grieco made his way down the corridor, ducking into a small storage closet near the floor's elevator lobby. He casually reached into a pocket, removed a cigar and lighter and lit up without snipping the tip off or removing the band.

Taking a deep breath of the acrid smoke from his Cuban, he reached into another pocket and retrieved his cell phone. He flipped it open and dialed.

"Mr. Tzi...yes, this is a private conversation. I have my cell on a scrambled network." He paused to listen. "Yes...yes, I have the information you wanted. Yes, I can meet you. No, I'll choose the location. Don't worry; I want this as badly as you, even more so maybe." He paused again. "Martin Street, the building site, tomorrow night, late." He grinned. "Fine, I'll be there."

He snapped the phone shut and took a lungful from his cigar, his smile never leaving his face.

* * * * * *

Leena sat in the study library, brooding in the leather wing chair normally reserved for Paul. Made from a beautiful antique brown Italian leather, and constructed from Australian hardwood by Australian chesterfield manufacturer Abbey Furniture, the chair had only recently arrived to replace one that had proven to be beyond repair.

Leena continued to brood. She hadn't heard from Paul in days and she was beginning to worry. She knew, of course, that Paul was trained for every eventuality, that he knew what he was doing above all else...but she worried nonetheless.

Has he stumbled upon something major? Has he been captured? And what about Max?

Despite her level head telling her there was nothing to be concerned about, her worst fears began creeping in to her train of thought, and the longer she heard nothing, the more prevalent such thoughts became.

"Will you be needing me anymore this afternoon, Miss?" said the butler, Jonathan Simpson, who had appeared in the library door.

"No, Simpson, I'm fine, thank you."

"I shall then begin to prepare the evening repast." Simpson turned to leave, but stopped and turned back to face her. He was a tall man with graying hair and piercing eyes. "Miss, are you all right? I know Master Paul and Master Max have failed to call in, but—"

"I just can't shake this feeling that something's wrong. Very wrong," Leena replied.

Simpson smiled in his own, gentle way and turned to leave. Leena remained seated, alone with her thoughts.

~ Chapter 9 ~

Stalemate. The Wraith, Max and Adam stood there, unable to move, their paths blocked by dozens of ninjas. The Wraith eyed his adversaries and calculated his next move carefully. This standoff wouldn't last much longer; he had to act quickly. To delay one more moment could cost them their lives.

A cry rang out, one of the ninjas signaling for his men to attack. The Wraith took action. He still had a capsule in his left hand, and he threw it to the ground at the feet of the oncoming horde, halting their sprint in a blinding flash of white light.

"Quickly, run!" The Wraith shouted. The trio did, dashing past the sprawled, screaming ninjas and into the forest. He wanted to get as far away from there as possible, and he knew they needed to make quick time after Blackova and Khan. Too much had already been lost.

"Where could they have gone?" The Wraith thought out loud, leading the charge through the dense forest. "They wouldn't have escaped on foot; they would have had an escape route planned from the start."

"But how? By air? There's no room to land a plane let alone take off," Max said.

"Wait a minute." Adam stopped. "What about a chopper?"

"But we heard nothing inside," Max said.

"No, he's onto something," The Wraith said. "I heard nothing from inside the building either, once we escaped the ninjas. The silence... The building was sound-proofed. Had to be."

Understanding registered on Max's face.

The Wraith came to a sudden halt. "We have to ascertain their flight path." He produced a tiny radio from his belt, a device so small and compact, yet so important under the current circumstances. "Leena? Leena, come in."

"Darling, thank God!" Leena exclaimed through the receiver.

"We're safe. Max is here. But I need you to check the radar scope. We're looking for a chopper crossing the western escarpment; I suspect it's traveling west. Get back to me as quickly as possible. Out."

"You think they're heading west?" Max asked.

"I doubt they'd be heading back toward Metro, and north or south both lead to more metropolitan areas. No doubt they have another base reasonably near here from where they can re-gather their forces. We can't give them that opportunity."

Adam looked perplexed, and not a little tired. "What can we do?"

"Do you remember the path you took to enter this valley?" The Wraith asked him.

"I think so, but we're on the other side of the valley. We'll need to hoof it to get there."

"Good. And how did you get into the mountains in the first place? By car?"

"Sure, I parked my jalopy in the brush, not far from the path—"

"Excellent," he interrupted. "We need to get there as quickly as possible."

The Wraith led them through the thick undergrowth. They had to make quick work of the several miles leading to the opposite end of the valley. Then they would be in Adam's hands, as he was the only one who knew of the secret path exiting this deep basin they were currently marooned in.

The Wraith continued to lead the way, running through the scrub, rounding trees and shrubs with great agility. Max followed closely behind. Despite his stocky stature, he was fit and, as The Wraith knew, had the determination to push himself beyond his own physical limits. Adam trailed the duo, slowing to a jog, clearly exhausted and ill-conditioned for such work.

"Keep up!" The Wraith shouted. "We cannot delay. The fate of so many lies with us."

At these words, Adam forced himself to quicken his pace, gaining some yards on Max, and the three continued their headlong drive through what on other occasions they would have recognized as some of the most beautiful country they'd ever seen.

The Wraith refused to allow his pace to slacken. His muscles were aching, his bones were weary, but he soldiered on.

The trio reached the plain located roughly within the center of the valley, and joined the path which ran adjacent to the small, winding brook.

"I know where we are," the Dread Avenger said, his pace never slowing. "We need to follow this path back into the forest ahead."

They were able to quicken their speed, having now reached the flat, open ground of the central heath. The Wraith glanced briefly behind him, and saw both Max and Adam were keeping a reasonable pace. Adam's face was flushed red through exertion, but the determination not to let the others down impressed the Dread Avenger, who determined there and then to make the young man a special offer once this was all done.

Once this is all done, The Wraith thought. *How confident that sounded.* He shrugged the feeling off. He had a job to do, and woe be to this country's citizens were he to fail.

They stopped in their tracks at the end of the trail, with the ground now starting to crest up into the trees.

"Straight up there" –The Wraith pointed– "is where I crashed my plane. It's steep country. We need to find the trail leading into this valley. Adam–"

Adam stepped forth, taking in his surroundings in an attempt to get his bearings. "This way." He pointed to the side. "We need to move along here, and then turn right."

"Are you sure?" asked Max.

Adam wasted no time; his reply was taking the lead and jogging in the direction he indicated. Their pace slowed some as Adam watched the path, lest he lead them astray. They slowly ran ahead of the wooded area; thorny blackberries riddled the ground where they trod, biting into their clothes and tearing into their flesh.

"Keep moving," The Wraith urged.

After a short but arduous trek along the wretched path, Adam stopped and again paused to scan the area.

"What is it? Is this the right way?" Max queried.

Adam furrowed his brow and slowly turned his head from one direction to another. "This way" —he pointed up into the trees— "I'm sure of it."

The Wraith looked to where Adam was pointing. The ground was much less rough there, but no less wooded. Thankfully, the blackberries ended where the sun was less prevalent on the ground.

"Let's go," The Wraith ordered. This time he took the lead, with Adam and Max close behind. Their tempo again accelerated, first up a gentle grade along what started as an often hard to discern path; then the path became more apparent, widening, confirming as the way out of the valley, but also signaling the start of a difficult climb to the top.

Adam stopped briefly to catch his breath; wheezing noticeably, he was clearly beginning to fade. The Wraith and Max stopped, and turned toward him. The hot sun was now low enough in the sky to be blocked by the surrounding cliff-face, giving them some respite.

"We must move on," The Wraith said. As he was about to continue, a soft, but audible, tone was heard emanating from his belt. He retrieved the radio from his belt. "Yes, Leena," he said and waited for a reply. "You're sure?" He paused. "Right. Hurry out here. We'll meet you on Highway 52 as soon as possible."

"News?" Max asked.

"They're heading west, as I suspected. Exactly where is anyone's guess, but once we get out of this valley, we'll make good time catching up."

"What?" asked Adam, still panting.

Max smiled his own understanding.

"How much further?" The Wraith asked Adam.

"Not far. You can see we're near the top, but the trail narrows and winds up ahead. We still have a ways to go."

Without saying another word, The Wraith bounded up the trail, the necessity of speed again taking hold of him, and Max and Adam could do nothing but follow as best they could. The grade became more precarious with each foot gained. The path soon narrowed, forcing them to slow and make the climb single file and pay close attention to each step taken.

Adjacent now to the towering cliffs, they scrambled over the rocky trail, making sure their footing was sound. The Wraith then inched along as the path narrowed even more. Then, with his back pressed against the cliff face, he rounded a corner.

"We're here, we've reached the top," The Wraith cried seconds later.

Max and Adam tried to hurry as best they could. They navigated the trail and turned into the crevice in the rock in which The Wraith had turned just moments before. Clambering along, The Wraith shot out a gloved hand from above them. Max grabbed it first, and was yanked up. The Wraith repeated the move, pulling Adam to safety atop the mountain.

"Phew!" Adam breathed heavily. "I never thought we'd make it." He paused, taking deep lungfuls of air. "What a view."

Not daring to delay any longer, The Wraith said, "Adam, where's your car?"

Still breathing heavily, he replied, "This way."

Following a small flat pathway, Adam led them toward a dusty clearing, where an ancient Ford was parked, covered with broken tangles of foliage in an attempt to shield it from view.

"Just in case I needed it again," Adam said. "I didn't want someone here to take off with it."

Max gave The Wraith a look which he instantly identified as "who would take this old bomb?" The Wraith dove in behind the wheel; Max and Adam got in the back. The car, surprisingly, started immediately. The Dread Avenger backed the car up, sending the branches careening off, wrenched the wheel about, and got the heap moving.

"She's a beauty, huh?" Adam said, smiling.

The road—if one could call it that—twisted and wound between trees and rocks. It was slow going, for The Wraith couldn't risk pushing the old car any harder, but at least they were making progress. A creek, which they forded, splashed water up over the windshield; the road on the other side widened considerably. For three miles, they traveled on before reaching what appeared to be a narrow, though bitumened, country lane.

"A mile that way" —Adam pointed to their left— "is the connection with Highway 52."

The Wraith gunned the car left, and hurtled it along as fast as the old Ford would go. Soon, they reached the highway.

"She should be here any minute," The Wraith said.

Acting almost as a reply, the sound of a small plane overhead caused the Dread Avenger to stamp hard on the brakes. The three exited the car and looked up. A compact but modern plane was coming down for a landing on the deserted highway in front of them—The Wraith's Falcon 900 private jet.

"Wow!" Adam said, amazed.

The Falcon 900 soon came to a halt, and Leena appeared at the side door. She lowered the staircase.

"The chopper is still moving west," she yelled.

The Wraith leaped up the stairs two at a time. He embraced the love of his life at the top.

"Darling," she said, kissing him briefly but passionately.

Max was next up the stairs, and he smiled broadly at Leena.

"Thank goodness you're okay, Max. I've been so worried," she said.

"You know me, I'm a tough nut to crack," the Irishman replied, and entered the craft.

"This is Adam," The Wraith said as the young man entered the plane. "He's been of immense help to us."

"Welcome aboard, Adam," Leena said. "Please take a seat, and we'll be on our way."

Adam could say nothing in reply, evidently amazed at the futuristic style of the plane's interior, The Wraith thought.

"Now the chase begins anew," The Wraith declared, as he hopped into the pilot's seat, and took over the controls. Leena sat beside him as his co-pilot. "Strap yourselves in. Let's go." The Wraith maneuvered the Falcon 900 down the highway, speeding up for takeoff.

* * * * * *

Sloan and Perez stood in Waldheim's office as a computer expert perused the hard drive files of the Chief Executive's computer.

"Still nothing," Sloan huffed, clearly annoyed with the progress of the investigation. "The factory's clean. This guy covered his tracks well."

"There's a chance we'll turn something up in the computer records," Perez said, hunched over the shoulder of the computer expert. "What do you think, Jim?"

"Well," Jim replied, "I haven't found anything out of the ordinary so far. Just the usual pay records, invoices, customer records, the...wait a minute...what's this?"

Sloan came up and hunched down behind the two to stare at the computer monitor.

"You see this?" Jim pointed at the records on the screen. "Someone's embezzled funds from the company retirement fund. You can see the figures don't match."

"Well, well," Perez said under her breath.

Sloan sniffed. "What does this prove, though, except that Waldheim was involved in de-frauding his own company as well as..."

"Wait," Perez added. "If Waldheim were stealing from the retirement fund...then why was he involved with these terrorists? It can't have been for the money. His salary must have been substantial. Plus, look at these figures—he must have been loaded."

Sloan carefully examined the figures on the screen again. "Hmm." He straightened and started to pace the office. "I have it," he finally said. "Whoever was responsible for the plague somehow found out about Waldheim's theft, and blackmailed him into acquiescence."

Perez eyed her partner closely. "That sounds plausible. We've seen in the past the lengths people will go for money and to save their own skins—but we can't prove it."

"You're right, but my gut tells me I'm on the money with this. Obviously the yogurt was the perfect place to spread the virus, and Waldheim's deceit suited their purposes to the letter."

"Save this to disc," Perez told Jim. "We'll present this to the commissioner, see what he thinks." She walked over to Sloan. "Even if you're right, this doesn't bring us closer to finding out the identity of those responsible."

"No, but it's a step closer, and it's more than I expected to find here, frankly," Sloan said. "C'mon guys, we're finished here."

~ Chapter 10 ~

The Falcon 900 continued west at high speed. The Wraith peered out his side-window; the lights from the myriad of farmhouses they passed over the only thing in sight. He turned to his instruments, then averted his gaze to Leena seated beside him.

"We're gaining on them," she said.

"Yes, but they have a massive head start on us and we may not be able to catch up with them before they land."

Night had fallen. The Dread Avenger's lips drew tight and hard against his teeth as he piloted the craft, determined. He worried that, despite their best efforts, Blackova and Khan would escape.

How would Metro City fare then? Or the country?

Blackova's ultimate plan was clearly not limited to his city alone. Her attempt to destroy the city was not only an attempt at revenge against him, but the start of her plan to finish what the Cobra had started. "The Cobra," he said under his breath.

What evil he had wrought upon my city. Even in death, the villain was causing havoc via his underlings. The Wraith swore right then to end this swiftly.

"Darling?" Leena said.

Before he could reply, he spotted something coming straight at them, and banked the plane sharply to the left, causing her body to press hard against her seat belt. After a moment, he righted the craft and Leena had composed herself. The Wraith briefly peered round into the rear of the plane. Max was still seated, protected by his seat belt, though winded—and coughing—from the experience. Adam was lying flat on the floor, stunned. The Wraith returned his attention to piloting the plane, while Leena then glanced back into the rear of the plane.

"Is he all right?" she asked Max. When assured thus, she then turned to The Wraith. "They're okay. Max has helped Adam back into his seat. What happened back there?"

"A missile, from somewhere up ahead," he said. "Our instruments failed to pick it up, and I only saw it myself at the last second."

Leena wiped her brow. The Wraith reached over, took her right hand in his left, and squeezed it gently.

"But how is that possible?" she said.

He couldn't reply, for he was veering the plane again, hard and to the left.

"What's going on?" she yelled above the whine of the engines.

"Plane coming toward us, bearing down on us!" The Wraith replied. "Leena, get back with the others. All of you strap yourselves in, emergency positions."

Leena immediately complied, moving carefully deeper into the plane. The Wraith knew she would direct Max and Adam to do as he told.

The Wraith gritted his teeth and held the controls of the plane tightly in his hands.

Not now, he thought, *not when we're so close to stopping those responsible for the plague.*

Fully alert, he saw nothing, but could make out the slight hum of an approaching plane. A second more, and he jerked the controls to his left. The opposing plane clipped the Falcon 900's right wing, snapping it off in a cacophony of engine noise and grating metal, but otherwise causing no further damage.

"Wing's damaged," The Wraith yelled above the racket. "We're going down. Hang on!"

The Wraith clutched the stick, using all his strength to keep the craft under some measure of control. He didn't have time to look out the window and inspect the damage properly, but he knew it was damaged enough to force the plane down. Just how they would get down was another question.

As they plummeted from the sky, the lights of the interstate came into view.

Thank the fates, The Wraith thought, *that Highway 52 is as straight as a runway at this location.*

He maneuvered the plane as best he could toward the highway. The plane shook violently, threatening to give way entirely, but he managed to keep it on course.

"Prepare for a crash landing!" The Wraith screamed. He only prayed the highway was deserted at this time of night because nothing could stop them from landing there now. Lowering the Falcon 900 as gently as possible took an intense effort of strength and will. He guided the damaged plane down, down toward the highway...the screeching of rubber hitting bitumen at high speed exploded in his ears with a foul screech. He was unable to slow the plane enough for a routine landing; he'd hit the ground too fast, with too much velocity. He pulled back on the brakes, hard. The front wheel snapped off, sending the front end of the plane smashing into the street, careening at high speed down the highway. What few cars there were managed to swerve to safety, allowing the plane to slide along its path along the interstate.

The Wraith grunted with the strain as he continued to apply his great strength to the brakes and to keeping the plane safely on the ground. Sparks shot up around the windshield, blinding the Dread Avenger momentarily. He relied on his sense of sound—the rending of metal on asphalt —to ensure he kept the plane on course.

After what seemed an eternity, the plane began to slow and, finally, came to a safe halt. Then, and only then, did The Wraith allow himself the luxury of breathing easy. He unlatched his harness, and rushed into the back of the plane.

"Everyone all right?" he called out.

Leena, Max and Adam were all safe, still in their seats and harnessed, though Adam appeared rather shell-shocked. Once The Wraith established the safety of his team, he unlatched the side door and quickly exited.

The plane was terribly damaged in the crash landing, but thankfully they had survived and no one else had come to harm in his forced landing on Highway 52. Leena soon appeared at the top of the stairs, exited the plane, and was followed by the others. They joined The Wraith in staring at the private jet.

There will be a reckoning, The Wraith vowed. *Yes, there will be a reckoning.*

* * * * * *

Back at Police Headquarters, Sloan and Perez were working late, trying to make sense of the senseless. Commissioner Harrison walked past them on his way out.

"It's late," Harrison said to both of them. "You can't work all night. Get some sleep."

"Yeah, in a minute," Sloan replied. "I'm just trying to get things straight in my head first."

Harrison stopped to join them. "What's there to work out? Waldheim was assassinated so he couldn't implicate those behind the plague."

"Sure, but...there's something else, something more," Sloan said.

"Like what?" Perez chimed in.

"I don't know, really—I just don't see those responsible being afraid of us, or being too afraid of us finding out more. They're too well organized for that, probably too vast to care. It pains me to say this, but I doubt a few cops could really dent their operation. Which leads me to think..." He paused to compose his thoughts.

"What?" Harrison prompted.

"To think there's more coming," Sloan finally said.

"More?" Perez said. "More what? Plague?"

After a pause to sigh, Sloan said, "I don't know. I honestly don't know."

* * * * * *

"I won't be able to repair this," Max declared, looking up at the sad sight of the plane. Smoke billowed out from somewhere beneath its nose.

"Umm...guys," Adam said, finally emerging from his shock. "We better get out of here. There's a bunch of cars coming." He pointed up the street, the smattering of lights confirming his statement.

"He's right, there'll be too many questions," Leena said. "We need to leave."

"First, I have to examine the wreckage," The Wraith said.

"Haven't we just done that?" Max asked, puzzled.

The Wraith took his eyes off the plane at last. "Not our plane; the plane that collided with us. It crashed some distance back."

"Holy—!" Max said. "You don't think..."

The Wraith ran from the street into the high grass of the adjoining pasture. "I need to see that plane."

The others joined him, dashing across the empty pasture. The long grass and, soon, the cover of a thinly forested grove covered their tracks. The Wraith produced a small, hand-held device from his belt, and before anyone could reach the Falcon 900, he pressed the button on it. The Falcon erupted in a massive ball of flame, completely destroying what was left of the private jet, taking its secrets to the grave.

Without breaking stride, they ran through the forest, The Wraith in the lead. Running for a thirty minute stretch, they arrived at the site of the other plane crash. The Wraith briefly eyed Adam, who had, surprisingly, kept up the entire way.

Impressive, he thought. He reconfirmed with himself to make the young man a special offer at a later date.

Wreckage was strewn over a fairly wide area and portions of it were still ablaze. The Wraith soon located the main fuselage and frantically looked for signs of survivors.

"Fighter jet," Max pointed out. "Expensive piece of hardware."

"Whoa," was all Adam could say.

Leena scurried about, helping The Wraith in his search; it was a fruitless endeavor. There was no sign of survivors–there was no sign of life at all.

"I can't find anyone," Leena said.

"There's no one to find. This plane was controlled by remote," The Wraith said, bending down. Despite it being somewhat crushed, he pulled what appeared to be a box with wires and a miniature antenna protruding from it from the smashed cockpit. He stood and held the device up for everyone to see.

"Then this means—" Max began to say.

"Yes. Blackova has escaped!" The Wraith said.

* * * * * *

As the sun began to creep over the Atlantic, signaling the beginning of a new day, Metro City embarked on the journey to recovery. With the plague situation at and end, the city was slowly springing back to life, or at least some semblance of normalcy. Newsstands began readying their stock for the morning rush, milkmen darted about, delivering their supply of dairy products to a hungry city, and even some of the hobos were already out asking for spare change.

As one milkman carefully planted a batch of milk on a particular doorstep, his morning reverie was shattered by a woman's scream erupting from within. Suddenly, the door flew open, and a lady of around fifty years of age appeared, frantic and blurry-eyed.

"I think my Bob's dead!" she screamed. "He won't wake up. Somebody help me!"

The milkman rushed in to see what he could do.

* * * * * *

Mick Jones shuffled along sleepily in his slippers. He always felt the worse for wear on Monday mornings.

How did that song go? he thought to himself, *I don't like Mondays. How apt.*

Work was a chore at the best of times, but Mondays just seemed to him to be cruel and unusual punishment. His wife was busily preparing the morning repast as he sidled up alongside her to give her a peck on the cheek.

"Morning, honey," he mumbled with half-open eyes. "That smells good."

His wife mumbled something in reply, and Mick slowly made his way to his side of the breakfast nook. He slowed, suddenly feeling weak and slightly dizzy.

"Marge?" he managed softly. "I don't feel so good."

His breath began to escape him and he started to pitch to-and-fro. He collapsed in a heap adjacent to the nook. Just barely conscious, he heard Marge scream in terror, as she rushed to his side and gently slapped him in the face to try and rouse him. He couldn't respond.

"Mick?—Mick!" she cried. Despite her frantic pleas, he remained still, with unconsciousness looming.

* * * * * *

The Metro City Police Headquarters was again a hive of frenzied activity. Reports were flooding in of men and women collapsing unconscious—possibly dead—mere minutes from waking. Nothing else was known at this early stage, but in the midst of the anarchy, Sloan and Perez entered the building, finding themselves once again in the center of a citywide maelstrom.

"What on Earth?" Sloan said upon seeing the state of his colleagues.

"Oh no," Perez said, sensing the urgency surrounding them. "You were right. More plague?"

"Let's see."

They dissected their work area and headed straight for the Commissioner's office. Briefly knocking, Harrison ushered them into chairs while he finished his phone conversation.

"Okay," Harrison started after placing the phone back on its cradle. "As you can see, we have a situation here."

"Not more plague, surely," Perez said frantically.

"It doesn't look that way, but it doesn't look good either. We have reports coming in from all over the city of people collapsing left, right and center."

"Dead?" she asked.

"Could be, judging by the early reports coming in. We have some officers over at some of the scenes; paramedics are struggling with those affected."

"Jeez!" breathed Sloan.

"Howard's already looking in on this, so you two head straight over there. I want the latest on what's affecting this city."

The two detectives exited Harrison's office in a hurry.

"What's going on here, Bob?" Perez asked.

"Your guess is as good as mine," he replied. "But this has to be the work of those responsible for the plague. Two disasters, one after the other—no way that's a coincidence. Let's go. I'm driving."

* * * * * *

Back home, Paul Sanderson sat uncomfortably in his library, in his usual wing chair, brooding. It galled him that his enemies had escaped; had, in fact, *toyed* with him in their escape. He and his team had survived, yes, but their quarry was still free. Free to cause more untold horror on the populace. Still, his enemies had allowed his team to survive—that was their mistake, and he vowed to make them pay by bringing them to justice.

While sitting alone, in silence, an insistent beeping roused him from his thoughts.

How long has it been beeping? he wondered.

With a quick glance to his Christopher Ward C60 Trident watch, the CW logo on the dial flashing confirmed an incoming call. Without further hesitation, he stood, produced a small remote control device from his pocket, and pressed the button on it. A section of the shelved wall pushed forward then parted, revealing the doorway to the Lair. He ran past the elevator, preferring the speed of the stairs, and soon reached the object of his headlong thrust—the communications terminal. With the flick of a switch, the beeping on his watch ceased. Paul pulled on a pair of headphones.

"Yes?" he said, pausing to listen. After a while, he said, "Understood. Out."

Max entered the Lair and stood facing Paul at the edge of the upper platform.

"Chief?" Max said, his voice not hiding his concern as he descended in the open-faced elevator.

"Max," Paul said, ashen-faced. "Get Leena. We're leaving— now!"

As Max reached the Lair's main level, Paul joined him and immediately sent the elevator back up. They returned to the library to find Leena rushing toward them.

"Darling, I've just heard from Sonya," she said.

"Astrid's daughter?" Paul said.

"Yes. Michael's dead."

"Quickly," Paul said. "If this is what I think it is, we have to get there as fast as possible."

* * * * * *

It was still early morning, but the sun was already well elevated, bathing the city in a deep orange glow which belied the situation Metro City once again found itself in.

Leaving Max in the car, Paul and Leena quickly strode up the driveway of their friends, the Lawson's. The family had recently been bereft with the death of Astrid, Leena's supervisor at work, and now it was apparent that disaster had struck the family again.

"And this has affected the entire city?" Leena asked as Paul knocked on the door.

Before he could reply, the door flung open, revealing Sonya's distraught form. Tears were streaming down her face, her makeup besmirched, and the bags under her eyes almost had a life of their own. Leena took her in her arms, consoled her. The pretty twenty-year-old seemed to appreciate it.

"It's okay," Leena said. "Tell us what happened." The three entered the small, but well furnished, inner city home.

"I...I...don't know. Dad got up as normal this morning, but collapsed on his way to the breakfast table," Sonya said, crying the entire time. "The paramedics are backed up. Apparently the same has happened elsewhere. I don't know what to do, I didn't know who to call."

"Where is Michael?" Paul asked.

"He's in the hallway. I didn't dare move him. I tried artificial respiration, but he didn't respond." Sonya broke down, and Leena again put her arm around her. She took her over to the sofa and sat down with her.

Paul found Michael's body where Sonya had indicated. He did indeed appear dead, and Paul closely examined him to make sure.

Yes, he thought, *he's dead*. He felt for a pulse. *Wait, is that a pulse?*

He bent over, pressed his ear to Michael's mouth. He was still breathing, but only barely, almost imperceptibly. His pulse was incredibly weak, virtually undetectable.

"Good Lord. Could it be?" Paul said quietly. *I need to make sure.*

Having had the foresight to come well equipped, he retrieved from his coat pocket a small syringe and carefully obtained a sample of Michael's blood.

"Leena!" he yelled. "We must get Michael to the hospital immediately."

Leena and Sonya quickly appeared at the end of the hallway.

"What is it?" Sonya asked.

"He's alive, though barely. If my assumption is right, he's been poisoned and needs emergency care if he's to survive this." Paul lifted Michael up and carried him past the girls to the door. "Quickly, we need to get him to a hospital."

* * * * * *

Sloan paced the floor of the City Morgue, with Perez watching on. They were waiting for Howard Boynce to appear, which he did moments later.

"Terrible," Boynce said, coming into the room.

"Oh no," Perez said in clear dismay.

"How many dead?" Sloan asked.

"None, actually," Boynce said.

"What?" Sloan said, shocked out of his pacing.

"No casualties. Those affected appear for all the world to be dead, but they're actually in a death-like state, complete catatonia."

"How is that possible?"

"I can guess, but we won't know for sure until we've finished our analysis, and even then, we may have to wait for results from head lab. You know how blessed we are with this 'fine facility.'" Boynce indicated around him. "I'm in constant contact with the city's hospitals. As soon as I know something—*if* I find out anything—they'll know it along with yourselves. At the moment, all patients are in a stable condition."

Sloan faced Boynce, eying him carefully. "So now what? We just sit back and wait?"

Boynce smiled at them wanly then rubbed his tired eyes. "We're performing tests as we speak. We may get lucky. I have a hunch, but we're working on a solution as fast as we can."

* * * * * *

Paul and Max were hunched over their equipment in the Lair's laboratory. Having gotten Michael to the hospital, they rushed back to home base to confirm, if possible, Paul's theory of the cause of this new affliction. Working feverishly, the duo were analyzing the blood sample from Michael Lawson, testing it for every known substance known to man, every ailment they were able to test for. Paul had his suspicions, but he had to know for sure. The hour that passed as they investigated seemed to take two.

Max, without moving an inch from his work, spoke up. "I wouldn't mind knowing how that Blackova lady could sway us like she did. For a while there, she was all I could think about. If not for your Judgment Stare..."

"Pheromones," Paul interjected.

"What?" Leena said, now joining the two in the lab.

"The closer Blackova came to us, the more intense the feelings of desire became," Paul said. Leena appeared concerned about this.

"You felt them too?" Max asked.

"From what I observed," Paul continued, "the closer she came, the longer she spent around us, the stronger the feelings we experienced...until eventually we started to lose control. I don't know how, but she seems to project pheromones the way female animals do while in heat to attract suitable males. Wait a minute—" After a pause, Paul raised his head from his microscope. "I was right. It *is* Zombie Powder."

"It's what?" Leena asked.

Paul ignored her, moved straight to the phone, and dialed Police Headquarters.

"Commissioner Harrison—this is The Wraith. Don't ask me how I got your direct number; don't ask me any questions, just listen. Those in the hospital afflicted earlier today have been poisoned." A pause. "Zombie Powder. Yes, that's right. They need to be given oxygen and drugs to regulate their blood pressure immediately. Trust me, it's not too late to avoid brain damage if you act quickly. Go!" And he hung up, not wasting any further time. "Thank God. I think we may have gotten to them in time."

"Okay, what's this about Zombie Powder?" Leena asked.

"It's a neurotoxin called tetradotoxin. TTX for short. Known as Zombie Powder in Haiti and areas of New Orleans."

"It rings a bell now," Max said. "From some fish, right?"

"Found in the ovaries of the puffer fish," Paul nodded. "The flesh of the fish itself is a delicacy in Japan, though it can be deadly if not prepared properly."

"But," Leena began, "how was it administered? Orally?"

"It's possible. The toxin is absorbed through the gastrointestinal tract, though there is another possible method of distribution."

"Which is?" said Leena.

"As a powder, the toxin can also be absorbed through the skin. It's common practice in Haiti for the powder to be sprinkled in a victim's shoes. Soon after exposure, they experience dizziness, shortness of breath and ultimately unconsciousness. Within about twelve hours, due to lack of oxygen to the brain—in essence, they become brain damaged—they become compliant, calm and controllable. It's used to control rowdy field workers in Haiti, also for certain voodoo rituals."

"That's awful," Leena said, her revulsion evident. "And this powder is freely available in the States?"

"I wouldn't say freely," Paul replied. "But it's certainly available in New Orleans, where I've encountered it before."

"That's right, you seemed to know it was Zombie Powder before we conducted these tests," said Max.

"I guessed, Max, though it was an educated guess based on past experience. I had to know for sure though. We're dealing with adversaries capable of any unspeakable horror. The wrong kind of treatment could have proven deadly. I had to know for sure." Paul walked over to the Lair's computer terminals.

"So, what's our next move, Chief?" Max asked.

"I doubt our enemy realizes we've discovered their latest poison as quickly as we have. We can use that to our advantage. It's late afternoon. Tonight, The Wraith prowls!"

~ Chapter 11 ~

Metro City was a different place at night. The day's legitimate businessmen and shoppers were replaced with hookers, pimps and lowlifes of every form. Now, with the city once again immersed in the terror of Natalya Blackova, the streets were deserted, lifeless except for the chill breeze which had started to pick up from the north.

Inside the open space of the building site on Martin Street, the breeze swirled, picking up the dust and litter strewn throughout. Charlie Grieco appeared from the shadows at the southern end of the site and pulled the collar of his coat up over his neck. He stood there a moment, pivoted from right to left, before lighting one of his favorite cigars. Extinguishing the match, he heard a noise up ahead of him. Drawing deeply from his Cuban, he watched and waited.

Ma Tzi soon emerged from the darkness across from him. Behind Tzi were three tall and burly bodyguards, eyeing Grieco carefully. Grieco stood there, smoking, calmly waiting for Tzi to meet him in the center of the pit.

"Ah, Mr. Grieco, pleasant evening, is it not?" Tzi called out, speaking in his usual gentle manner.

"Umm...yeah," was all Grieco could reply.

Tzi stopped several feet in front of him, guards directly behind Tzi. "I see you are ready to do business. May I see the papers?"

Grieco reached inside his coat, causing the guards to reach to their gun belts in anticipation of a potential threat. "Cool it, okay," he said, as he slowly pulled a manila folder from his coat. "Do you have the money?" He handed one of the papers to Tzi for inspection.

Tzi pointed to the guard to his left, who opened the leather briefcase he was carrying, and revealed wads of greenbacks. "Five hundred thousand, as we agreed."

"And a position of power within your organization," Grieco added.

"But of course," Tzi said, smiling. "Shall we trade?"

The guard handed the briefcase to Tzi, who then placed it on the ground in front of him. Grieco then did the same with the folder.

"As you can see, this information will allow you to put a severe dent in Latham's immediate business plans, causing enough damage to seriously undermine him. You can then pounce on his partners, taking Latham down through attrition alone."

Tzi smiled with apparent glee as he reached down to retrieve the folder. As he did so, the guard to his left produced a pistol from his gun belt, and fired into his boss's back. Instantly, the assassin turned, firing at the guard nearest to him, killing him instantly. The third guard, in shock, tried to reach for his weapon, but was taken down by Grieco's powerful gun. It was all over in seconds.

Tzi, still alive—barely—attempted to crawl away. Blood spread from his wound, coating his back. Grieco and the rogue guard watched on, but remained still. Behind them, a figure appeared from the safety of the shadows—Robert Latham. He ambled past his two men, up beside his enemy and rolled Tzi over with his foot. Tzi looked up at the crime lord, grimacing.

"You—" Tzi hacked, blood leaking from the corners of his mouth.

Latham placed his right foot on Tzi's chest and pressed down, causing Tzi to cry out in pain. "Did you think I would just let you have *my* city without a fight? Did you think my 'feeble' attacks on your stronghold was all I was capable of?"

Latham's eyes glowed with a mix of anger and triumph. He looked as though he was about to continue, but suddenly changed tack, pulling out a pistol of his own, firing once into Tzi's head. He fired again, into the corpse's torso. And again. And again. Latham shrieked in primeval triumph. Finally, his vengeance sated, Latham dropped his gun on the ground beside the body. He reached up and casually smoothed his hair back into position.

"Take care of this mess, Charlie," he said, and walked back toward the shadows from whence he came.

As the clouds parted, revealing an incandescent, almost-full moon, Grieco looked at the guard with an expression that the guard returned with interest, then turned to view the blood-stained body of the former "Dragon of Hong Kong." Grieco had long known of Latham's ferocity against his enemies. He'd seen such examples with his own eyes, had participated in his own samples of brutal violence at Latham's orders. He was also well aware of Latham's ascendancy to power as a young man, albeit mostly second and third hand. But this was the first time he had seen such darkness coming from Latham himself, and while he had long ago been desensitized to such violence, this incident had put his own quest for power into a new perspective. His thirst remained as strong as ever, and he hoped that this sign of loyalty would quell any doubts Latham may have had in him, but he would now have to be very careful in his future planning. *Very* careful indeed.

* * * * * *

The moon had reached its zenith in the night sky, illuminating the city in a hue almost supernatural in its brilliance. The Wraith crept along the enlarged ledge of a twenty two storey luxury apartment block on Metro's inner west side, trying to position himself for a better view at the proceedings up on the rooftop to his left.

The Wraith carefully raised his head and peered over the brick partition. While on patrol, he'd noticed a couple of cat burglars staking out their next target. He'd hated being diverted from his main task, but crime never seemed to take a break in Metro City.

"Careful now," said the taller of the two men. "That cabling cost us a fortune."

"Yeah, yeah. I know what I'm doing," the shorter man replied.

Both were outfitted in dark, heavy-duty work outfits with night-vision goggles snapped to their heads. The shorter man carried an intricate, miniature cable-and-pulley system, designed to lower and raise a person from great heights—

essential equipment for any professional cat burglar. The taller man appeared to be the leader of the duo, and also appeared rather impatient.

"This is the last building for tonight, so let's get to it," the taller man said.

"Look, this takes careful positioning," the shorter man replied. "What's with you tonight? What's with the attitude? We've done this a million times before."

The taller man sighed. "I don't know. I just feel a menace in the air tonight. I just want to get this over and done with as quickly as possible."

The smaller man stopped, patted his comrade on the shoulder. "Ralph—it's just the craziness this city has been going through the last week. It's nothing. C'mon, like you say, let's get this over with. This building has treasures just waiting for us to plunder."

The two thieves moved over to the building's edge. The smaller man planted the pulley system at a select spot and lowered the support struts, which Ralph then bolted into place. The two pulled some slack into the cables, readying to attach it to their belts. As Ralph tested the strength and integrity of the cabling, the smaller man moved to gaze over the edge, searching for the perfect position to rappel downwards. What he found instead, was the face of the Dread Avenger of the Underworld staring right at him.

"Yahhh!" the shorter man cried.

In an instant, The Wraith vaulted onto the rooftop and delivered a powerful blow to Ralph's solar plexus, rendering him inactive and gulping for breath. The shorter man tried his best to escape capture, tried to go on the attack, but he was ill-skilled and a quick one-two punch from The Wraith ended the battle before it had begun. Ralph rolled around in pain, desperately trying to get his breath back, but was unable to act in time. The two thieves were quickly ensnared, ready for pickup by the police as soon as they were alerted of the thieves' presence.

The Wraith stepped back over to the edge of the building. He hoped these interludes—this had been the third already tonight—would not distract him from his real task—finding those responsible for the spread of the Zombie Powder. He felt certain he held an advantage over Blackova and Khan—for it was surely they who were responsible for this latest attack—felt sure they would be unaware of his quick discovery of the powder. He had to make that advantage work for him, even if it took all night. He pulled from his belt his powerful mini-binoculars, and scanned the area. Nothing out of the ordinary, nothing to indicate any illicit activity.

He decided to move to higher ground, somewhere more centrally located to gain the best and widest possible view of the inner city. The newly constructed Latham Industries building fit the bill. The Wraith launched himself from the roof, using his cape as a parachute. Latham Industries was blocks away, and he needed to move fast.

* * * * * *

In a darkened room, a tall, broad, robed figure moved silently forward through the cloudy darkness as though floating instead of walking. It moved silently and gently through the room toward a thin slice of light at the opposite end. Reaching it promptly, the figure raised an arm clad in tattered rags, revealing a skeletal hand.

Pointing to a photo of Robert Latham tacked to the wall, the sinister robed figure said, "You will pay for your sins, Robert Latham. Your importation and presentation of our most sacred artifact is a sin so great that it cannot—*will not*—be ignored."

The figure leaned in close to examine the photo of Latham. He breathed heavily. His face was hidden by a tatty, filthy brown hood, part of the tattered robes that covered his body from head to toe; his skeletal hands were the only part of his body visible, protruding from gaping sleeves.

"Your day is coming, Latham," the figure grumbled. "And soon."

The figure grabbed a ceremonial dagger from the shelf under the photo, raised it aloft, its blade gleaming in the silver moonlight. The figure then plunged the dagger into the photo, embedding the blade deep in the wall, right through Latham's head.

"*Very* soon!"

* * * * * *

The night sky had clouded over with the thickness of an impending storm. There was already a soft rumbling in the clouds, and the wind had picked up considerably. Now positioned atop the almost-complete new Latham Industries building, The Wraith stood on a widened section of the surrounding scaffolding, watching, waiting. He scrutinized his city through his mini-binoculars; their night-vision capabilities lit up even the darkest of alleys. An incoming call registered in The Wraith's cowl. The soft beeping was interrupted by The Wraith tapping at his right temple.

"Yes?"

"Chief, nothing out of the ordinary here so far. Leena and I will continue our patrol," Max said.

"Understood."

Doubt began to creep into the Dread Avenger's mind. *Perhaps I was meant to discover the source of the city's latest malaise as quickly as I did? Was this merely a ruse to divert my attention from a larger, more complex scheme?* He lowered his binoculars, that latter thought now dominating everything else. *A ruse, a diversion from something else, something worse?*

The shrill sound of a whistle being blown–subtle, almost inaudible amongst the reverberation of the building maelstrom in the skies above–caught The Wraith's attention. He stared through his binoculars, trying to find the source of the whistle. His cape billowed around him, the wind buffeting him, causing him to check his footing. "Where are you dammit!" he cursed under his breath. *There!* In an alley a short distance away, there was movement. Through his night-vision binoculars, The Wraith was able to make out several figures scuttling about quickly. *Ninjas!* This was it, the breakthrough he had anticipated.

He intended to make the most of it.

* * * * * *

With the sky illuminated in lightning and crashing thunder, the ninjas hurried along their path through the alley. The ninja leading the procession turned to face his oncoming troupe. He produced a small, thin whistle and blew it. The troupe responded in turn, congregating before the leader in quick, and exact, fashion.

"Do not fail in your sacred mission," the ninja leader said. "Our mistress has honored us and we must repay that great honor with the success she demands of us."

A lightning bolt crashed overhead, illuminating the alleyway in a quick, sharp flash of light. There, behind the ninja leader, stood the Dread Avenger of the Underworld, his cape outstretched in a vision of vampiric menace, his face contorted in severe fury. The troupe of ninjas gasped at The Wraith's shocking appearance, causing the ninja leader to pivot.

"Hear me now!" boomed The Wraith as the rain began to fall. "Your wickedness ends tonight!"

* * * * * *

With a scream of defiance, the ninja leader launched himself at The Wraith. The Dread Avenger parried the attempted blow, and caught the leader's leg at his next attack, and threw him against the building wall to the right, stunning him. Two more entered the fray. The Wraith stepped forward, grabbed the ninja to his left and in a lightning-fast move, swiveled, using the hapless ninja as a shield against the attack of the second, who had produced a deadly set of nunchakus. The Wraith dropped the wounded warrior to the ground. The rain pelting down, the ninja brandishing his nunchaku flipped his weapon in an attempt at skilled showmanship. The Wraith lashed out with a powerful kick to the head, ending the contest in a split-second.

The Wraith growled in rage as three more ninjas surrounded him, ready to attack. They assailed in unison, fists and feet flying with prodigious skill and power. The Wraith ducked a spinning scissor kick from one ninja, hopped above the leg sweep from another, and blocked a karate chop from the third with his wrist gauntlets. The Dread Avenger lashed out, backhanding the third ninja into a series of trash cans lining the alley wall. The second ninja took advantage of this and connected with a kick to The

Wraith's stomach. More surprised than stunned or hurt—for his costume bore the brunt of the assault—The Wraith nevertheless lost concentration for a moment. And a moment was all the ninjas needed.

The first ninja chopped into the back of The Wraith's neck, causing the Dread Avenger to cry out. The second ninja executed a perfect spinning side kick, his foot smashing into the side of The Wraith's head. The Dread Avenger toppled, splashing into the engorged puddle now building up in the central section of the alley. The rain still tumbled down.

Exaltations of triumph erupted from the two ninjas; the sight of The Wraith on his knees, panting, no doubt encouraged them. The Wraith gritted his teeth, noting the ninjas' failure to attempt to finish him off.

Big mistake, he thought.

Enraged, the Eyes of Judgment began to glow and crackle with concentrated, mystical energy. The memory of the incredible destruction wrought by the Cobra and now his minions re-fueled the Dread Avenger's weary body. He stood, his muscles tensed, his body rigid and ready for action. One of the ninjas charged fiercely. The Wraith backed up against the building wall nearest him, then jumped up and latched onto the bottom rung of a fire escape. The Wraith wrapped his legs around the hapless ninja's head, and squeezed. The ninja hacked and squirmed as best he could, but he was helpless in the Dread Avenger's thrall. The Wraith waited for the optimal moment then spun the ninja like a top in the air. The warrior landed face first into the hard alley floor, avoiding the relative safety of the ever-growing puddle at the center of the alley.

The Wraith dropped to the ground, hunched over, ready to finish this battle as quickly as possible. The remaining ninja didn't waste any time and attacked immediately. The

Wraith dodged a roundhouse punch then delivered a powerful uppercut to the jaw. The resultant sickening crack could only have been the sound of teeth shattering. The ninja staggered backwards, rubbing his jaw gingerly. The Wraith decided to press on with his attack. The ninja hurdled forward only to find The Wraith taking him down with a spinning sweep kick to the legs. On his back, the ninja still tried to attack The Wraith, pulling from his belt a shuriken. The Wraith kicked it from his hand. Crouching down, The Wraith punched the ninja hard on the nose, breaking it and sending him to sleep.

The Wraith stood and allowed himself a deep breath. The battle was won. Then two more ninjas standing at the rear of the alley, protected as they were by the shadows of the surrounding buildings. He faced them—and the ninjas ran. Rounding a corner, they were gone in an instant. The Wraith turned to size up the situation. There were several battered warriors lining the alley floor, all outfitted in the usual black, soft-linen fabric and design unique to the ninja warrior. Each had a small bag clipped to their belts. The Wraith crouched down beside one of them and placed a finger into the bag. He withdrew it.

Powder, obviously Zombie Powder. He'd stopped them in the middle of disseminating more of the dreaded poison.

The Wraith stood, thankful he'd been successful and evermore determined to end the evil posed by Natalya Blackova. All the ninjas were still unconscious save for the troupe leader, who was only now beginning to awaken.

Perfect. Now for some answers.

The Wraith yanked the ninja up and ripped the warrior's mask from his head. His sandy, full hair flopped down over his forehead. Well trained in martial arts they may have been, but true ninjas they were not. The Wraith noted the peculiarity of the ninja's eyes—fogged over and hazy in color.

"I want answers—Now!" The Wraith demanded.

Nothing. The leader remained silent, evidently bewitched by Blackova's charms. The Wraith plunged his fist into the ninja's stomach, then pulled him straight once again.

"Answers!"

"I...I will tell you nothing," the ninja coughed.

The Wraith smashed his fist into the thug's face. He reached up, seized a solid handful of the ninja's hair, and jerked the unfortunate warrior's head down into the gaze of the Eyes of Judgment, which were once again crackling with ferocious energy.

"You who have sinned," The Wraith roared, "you who have created such fear, such destruction of life—now feel the fruits of your trespasses!"

The ninja struggled with as much strength as he could muster, trying to avert his gaze. But it was for naught. Once caught in the web of The Wraith's Judgment Stare, there was no escape. The ninja leader's face contorted in pain then in complete mental anguish as all his sins, the pain he'd spread to others, washed over him in an instant. He screamed in agony. The Wraith let him drop onto the puddle beneath them. The rain kept coming down.

Partially submerged in the ever increasing pool, the ninja began rambling incoherently.

Or is he?

The Wraith snatched the ninja up; the warrior made no other sound save that of his mumblings.

"Tell me, what are Blackova's plans?" The Wraith said.

"The president...the president..." the ninja wheezed. "World's Fair..."

The Wraith jerked the ninja forward, growling in the ninja's face. "The president? She's targeted the president? At the World's Fair?"

The ninja faltered; his body became limp in The Wraith's arms, unconsciousness beckoning. "Yes..." he managed to utter before dropping to the ground.

The Wraith quickly checked for a pulse. It was slow and steady; he was fine.

The wind picked up. A tremendous thunder clap, instantly followed by a fierce lighting strike nearby, could not shake him from this terrible revelation—Natalya Blackova planned to assassinate the US president!

~ Chapter 12 ~

The Dread Avenger stormed into the Lair, Max and Leena close at his heels. The three were drenched from the rain, but none noticed nor cared. They had bigger things to worry about.

"Leena, contact Harrison, let him know there may have been more Zombie Powder infections tonight, but that the band responsible were stopped," The Wraith said. "Max, get onto the weather system. I need to know if I can take off immediately."

"I can tell you right now the weather's too treacherous for any kind of air transport," Max warned. "You'd have to go and 'borrow' another plane anyway. No-go." He moved over to the massive computer terminal, appearing to double check.

Leena pressed up against The Wraith. "Darling, do you think it's really possible that the president is Blackova's target? To what end?"

"She shares the Cobra's mantra—to conquer."

"But what would she truly achieve?"

"Chaos. Anarchy. Perhaps she has men positioned in places of influence, ready to take advantage of such a situation. Max and I have both seen firsthand the power she yields over men."

"Chief," Max called. The Wraith and Leena strode over to him. "The weather is getting worse. Winds are now up to one hundred miles an hour. Emergency services are dealing with damage throughout the city. A dozen lightning strikes have been reported. We're not flying anywhere."

The Wraith spun on his heels. "Damn! President Atworth is officially opening the World's Fair in Philadelphia tomorrow at 11 A.M. That's when Blackova will surely strike. I need to get there as quickly as possible."

"Chief." Max spun in his chair. "The car. We can drive there."

"*I* can drive there...of course. Max, is it ready? It hasn't been tested yet," The Wraith said.

"It's as good a time as any," he replied with a wink. "But you're not going alone."

"No, we need to—" Leena began.

"You and Max need to stay here. There may yet be groups of ninjas remaining. You need to find them and neutralize them."

The Wraith didn't waste any further time and marched over to the Lair's elevator. Together they rode it to the upper platform. With his team in tow, they entered the library, almost bumping into Simpson, who was heading for the Lair.

"I heard the beeper, sir. I knew somebody was home. I was coming down to see if you required any assistance tonight," said Simpson.

"No, thank you, you can get back to sleep," The Wraith said.

The three moved past Simpson with a purposeful stride, exiting the library and moving silently through a corridor, then another shorter one, before finally entering the expansive garage where Paul Sanderson parked his numerous cars. Sports cars, antique rides, sedans—all expensive. Rounding the Mercedes, the BMW, the Aston Martin, and the Bentley, the trio arrived at the far end of the garage and came face-to-face with Paul's newest vehicle—the very expensive Bugatti Veyron. Over a million dollars of state of the art automobile, 8.0L 16 cylinder engine, top speed of nearly 280mph, which it could achieve in only 55 seconds—and those were just the basic specs. Since purchasing the very exclusive car, Max had tinkered with it a little in his spare time. Tests on the enhanced vehicle had yet to take place, so its capabilities could only be estimated.

"Okay, Max, find out the president's schedule—to the second. I need to know where he is, where he will be and when," The Wraith said. "Leena, you get out on patrol. There's still much of the night left, and the police will need help finding those ninjas, if there are any left."

The Wraith slipped behind the wheel, the cockpit resembling that of a modern aircraft, with its mottled metallic silver console and aerodynamic styling. Max leaned over the open car door.

"Everything is self-explanatory, the cockpit is perfectly designed to help you stay focused on the road and not on peripheral controls," Max said. "When you want to reach top speed, press the Speed Key button here." He indicated its position between the seat and the sill. "That will retract the rear wing and spoiler, the front diffuser panels will close and the ride height will drop, causing less drag and faster speeds.

And" —he pointed to a small button underneath the gear stick— "this button will increase your speed even more."

"By how much?" The Wraith asked.

"A lot. I can't give you a closer estimate, but I'd advise you to use that only in an absolute emergency. The car wasn't built for speeds above its maximum. I can't be sure the car will hold up under the strain."

Leena appeared concerned with the way the two men were talking.

Softening his voice and expression, The Wraith said, "I'll be okay, darling. Just keep your mind on the mission. If we fail..." He stopped, the thought too difficult to entertain.

"We won't fail." Leena was adamant.

The Wraith started the engine, its roar deafening in the confined space of the Sanderson garage. Max slammed the car door shut, but as The Wraith began to edge the car through the garage, he mouthed the words "I love you" to Leena through his window. And then, with a roar, he was gone.

* * * * * *

Figures scurried through the pitch darkness, the only sound to be heard were that of their feet trudging across the floor. After a few moments, a weak light was switched on, revealing the interior of a large tent, akin to a circus big top, where several ninjas rushed about, some carrying intricate pieces of electronic equipment, others vials containing unknown substances. Pushing aside an awning, the imperious Magnus Khan entered. He held the cloth open, allowing Natalya Blackova to follow. She was again outfitted in a sexy, body-hugging outfit made from the finest black silk.

"Mistress." Khan bowed. "Work is progressing on schedule."

"And The Wraith?"

"No doubt dealing with the new spate of poisonings in the city, no doubt perplexed as to your grand plans," Khan said.

"No doubt," Blackova said. "Perhaps we can be more certain of the situation?"

Khan got the message. "Yes, Mistress." And he rushed back from whence he came, visibly eager, as ever, to do her bidding.

Blackova strolled amongst her busy minions, carefully watching as they performed their duties. She smiled. Yes, The Wraith had proven more resilient than she had anticipated. She never contemplated he would have survived, let alone having escaped her clutches in her valley stronghold. *No matter*, she thought. While she was forced to accelerate her plans somewhat, her ultimate goal remained attainable.

"And then," she said to herself, "once the World's Fair, and the president along with it, have been destroyed, and my power consolidated—then I will finally wreak vengeance upon The Wraith and all those he cares about!"

* * * * * *

The Bugatti Veyron sped through the city, weaving through the traffic like a NASCAR racer homing in on the finish line. The Wraith maneuvered the high-powered automobile with the skill of Mario Andretti in his prime, gaining speed where he could, but being forced to slow down at times behind traffic, which was now starting to build up in this part of the city and which he temporarily could not avoid.

He ground his teeth in frustration. The rain was pelting down with as much force as ever, and the wind was fierce; he veered the car into a narrow side street, smashing through a series of full trash cans in an attempt to bypass the building quagmire of city traffic. He yanked the wheel left. The car slid wildly, but he managed to regain control of the vehicle in quick time, enabling him to re-enter traffic, which was significantly lighter there. He pushed the car as hard as he could within the city speed limits and within the current weather conditions. He had to get out of the city as quickly as possible, for he could make much greater time on the freeways connecting Metro City with Philadelphia.

While The Wraith was concentrating on keeping control of his powerful vehicle, the sound of sirens could be heard approaching from the rear. The Wraith checked his rear-view mirror and saw at least three police cars pursuing him. He cursed the fates.

The fools! If they stop me, all hope is lost.

He pressed down on the gas, deciding the best course of action under the circumstances would be to outrun the police. The car accelerated and while traffic was indeed lighter here, it was still extant, and the Dread Avenger had no wish to cause harm in his furious quest to save the president. The police continued their pursuit and managed to gain back some of their lost ground.

"Dammit!" The Wraith said.

It was clear the authorities would not give up. In fairness, how were they to know this speeding car contained the Dread Avenger of the Underworld? How were they to know that by stopping him, they threatened the very fabric of this country's way of life? The Wraith had no time for fairness;

only action remained. Keeping one hand on the wheel, he pressed a point at his temple, activating his cowl's radio.

"Chief?" came Max's immediate response.

"The police are pursuing me. I don't have time to deal with them nor the potential harm their chase may cause innocents. I need Leena to contact Harrison, tell him to call off his men—Now!"

The Wraith switched his radio off without waiting for a reply. He sped up again, and within the next few minutes, the police cars slowed and vanished from sight.

Leena's done it, he thought. *Good.*

The Dread Avenger swerved the Bugatti sharply, just catching the entry into the Metro-Philadelphia freeway. A small smile curled on his lips. *Finally*, he thought, and stepped on the gas as far as it could go. The rear spoiler retracted and the car lowered on its axles. It was a race he could not afford to lose.

~ Chapter 13 ~

The weather had not relented. Visibility was poor and the rain lashed at The Wraith's windshield. He had left Metro City behind and was making good time, pushing the car up to 250mph, but the conditions were precarious, and the wind harsh in its intensity. In these dreadful conditions, he dared not push the car any further.

He continued plowing through the weather as fast as he could. His thoughts turned to the Cobra; the vile, evil menace that attacked Metro City the previous year. What destruction he had wrought. The monster had turned Metro into his own personal killing field. The Cobra had died in the struggle. Now his underlings had caused even more death, even more heartache. The Wraith made a solemn vow to end this tonight.

The beeping of an incoming call on his in-cowl radio interrupted his train of thought.

"Yes?" The Wraith said.

"Chief, the president is staying at the Ritz-Carlton Hotel on George Street. He has no appointments in the morning before formally opening the World's Fair at 11:30 A.M."

"Excellent," he said. "Then it's imperative I reach him at the Ritz-Carlton before he leaves for the fair. He's sure to leave at least an hour or two before the opening ceremony, so that gives me" —he checked the clock on the car's dash— "roughly five to six hours to stop this travesty from happening." The seriousness of his situation hit him hard. It would be touch-and-go reaching Philadelphia in time, and then he had to formulate a plan to reach the president; to warn him, save him. "Good work. Now, you and Leena hit the streets again. There's only a little over an hour left of darkness; if there are any ninjas left, I want them stopped. Out."

The Wraith felt a swelling of pride for his team. His crusade against injustice had taken him all over the world, had prompted him to make great sacrifices in his life—but he had also gained so much and, he hoped, had helped make the world a better place.

The rain relented ever so slightly and he prayed it would ease some more. The storm itself had since wavered; there had been no sign of any lightning strikes for a good half hour or so. And, better yet, the wind had also abated considerably. He dared to hope this was the break in the storm he had been praying for. He decided to push on as he was, but at the slightest further sign of improvement in the weather, he would thrust the car toward its 280mph maximum speed and, if required, beyond.

* * * * * *

Leena looked at Max, concerned. She regretted once again being unable to be by Paul's side during this crisis, but she also knew he had entrusted her and Max with an important mission, and she was determined to succeed. She knew, like Max and Simpson, the importance of working together as a team, for their safety had often depended on their individual skills and intelligence coming together.

Leena headed to the wall lined with a myriad of Wraith costumes, some of which were her own, specially designed to disguise her femininity, making her appear to all the world— at least from a distance or from the shadows—as The Wraith himself. She had been able to mimic the Dread Avenger's voice through the aid of a small device devised by Max and placed in the neck of her costume, and had often stood in for The Wraith when the situation called for it (like when confronting Latham and meeting with Harrison earlier).

"We need to show Blackova that we haven't caught on to her scheme, and the best way to do that is for The Wraith to continue to be seen tonight, here in Metro City," she said.

She pulled the cowl from its stand and looked at briefly, thoughtfully. It was time to go into action.

* * * * * *

Nightshifts were usually the busiest for Metro City cops; Sloan and Perez were out on patrol. Sloan looked annoyed.

"I know why you're acting this way," she said to him as she drove the two of them through the inner city.

"And why am I acting this way?" he fired back.

"You don't like the fact that Commissioner Harrison has been...taking advice...from The Wraith."

"He's a damn vigilante, works outside the law, and we're taking the word of the likes of him?" Sloan's face was already red.

"I don't know," she said. "Maybe things aren't as simple as that. The world isn't as black and white as you think. Maybe this Wraith character is on the level. You have to admit, he hasn't let us down yet."

"You make a good case." He sighed. "But I remember this city before we had armed vigilantes patrolling the streets, before crime made Metro its capital." He sighed again. "Maybe we'll see those days again."

As Perez turned the car onto a side street, their unmarked was suddenly peppered with gunfire, bullets plowing into the side doors. Perez slammed on the brakes, skidding the car to one side.

"Jeez, we're under attack!" shouted Sloan as the two cops ducked. He opened the passenger door and wriggled out onto the wet street. He quickly urged Perez to follow him. They hunched behind their car, waiting.

"What the hell have we stumbled into?" Perez whispered, brandishing her gun.

"I don't know, but they picked the wrong night to try and whack me." Sloan wrenched his gun from its holster and held it up.

Perez carefully peered through the car's windows, and what she saw horrified her. What appeared to be a band of ninjas—for they were clad in the familiar garb of the ancient Japanese warrior—were marching down the street, waving uzis, firing indiscriminately into shop fronts, cars, mailboxes–and at anything that moved.

"We have to call for backup," Perez said. "People are being slaughtered, and there must be at least a dozen perps headed our way."

Bullets again slammed into their car, causing Perez to block her ears from the noise. Fortunately their vehicle was protecting them.

"We'll be cut down if we make a break for it," Sloan said. "We have to try and hold them off and pray backup arrives in time."

He rocketed to his feet, reached over the car and fired three shots, before hurriedly dropping back down to safety. Perez was busy calling it in.

"I think I got one," he said after she had finished. "How are we with ammo?"

"We have enough to last a short time, I think. Help's on its way."

"Good," he said quickly, firing again into the group of ninjas, taking another two down. Perez followed suit, felling two ninjas of her own. The two cops hit the ground fast as gunfire again came their way, bullets drilling into their car and whizzing above their heads. Both tires on the side of the car facing the ninjas blew out, as did the windows, showering them with shards of glass. The car began to resemble a piece of scrap metal from a wrecker's yard.

"We plugged a few more, but there are more bringing up the rear," she said.

"Give me some shells. I'm out. Dammit, where's that backup?" he said.

"It's here," a familiar voice said behind them.

* * * * * *

Sloan and Perez whirled around and came face-to-face with Leena dressed as The Wraith. Leena had her cloak wrapped around her. "Stay down," she said in The Wraith's voice, and the two cops, stunned, did so.

In a lightning fast move, Leena vaulted the car, landed deftly in a crouch, executed a sidewards roll and avoided the barrage of bullets before lobbing several gas pellets into the pack of ninjas. A thick smoke enveloped the black-clad warriors, concealing them from view. She dived into the chaos and took advantage of the ninjas' confusion. Lashing out, she kicked and punched with force, dealing with each warrior in turn, quickly, savagely. In the few minutes it took for the smoke to clear, Leena was able to defeat the entire horde. She stood above their unconscious bodies lying in a heap around her, her cape wrapped around her.

"Jeez!" was all Sloan could say, having emerged from his hiding spot. Perez rounded the car and walked over to Leena.

"Those weren't ninjas," Leena said, stopping Perez in her tracks. "Ninjas don't carry automatic weapons. They were a mere diversion to ensure we were kept bogged down in Metro City."

"What's that you say?" Sloan said, having joined Perez on the other side of the ruined car. "A diversion? From what?"

The three were interrupted by the shrill sirens of approaching police cars arriving en masse. Sloan twisted and waved his hands, trying to signal the approaching cops to switch their sirens off. When he turned back around–Leena had gone. She saw his puzzlement from a neighboring rooftop.

* * * * * *

The Bugatti Veyron hurtled down the freeway at its top speed of 280mph. Traffic was still light and The Wraith was able to weave through what there was with ease. The car handled perfectly, and he silently thanked Max for having ensured its roadworthiness. Dawn could only be minutes away, and he had to reach Philadelphia as quickly as possible. He knew he would have to ditch the car just within the city limits, so reaching that point swiftly became evermore essential in increasing his available time on foot.

Thankfully, the rain had now completely stopped, and the wind died down to a mere breeze. The road was already nearly dry and the journey grew smoother by the second. The Wraith began to hope against hope that all obstacles had been surmounted, and that he'd have a relatively free ride from here on in.

He passed a street sign—Philadelphia was now only a few miles away. However, his free ride was rudely shaken when he saw a stream of Philadelphia police cars tailing him.

"Damn, not again," he grumbled. He knew they couldn't be called off the way his own city's officers could, and he didn't have the luxury of driving off-road to lead his pursuers on a merry wild goose chase. No. This had to be a quick evasion. But how?

The answer was presented to him as the sight of a police road block loomed before him. *What now?* He couldn't be captured, not with so much at stake. He briefly thought of punching through the barricades, but almost instantly thought better of it. The car wouldn't survive the impact and he still had to get into the city. Then it came to him—the button under the gear stick. Max had told him it would increase his speed by a large margin. *Enough to jump those barricades?* The Wraith could only hope.

The Dread Avenger neared the point of no return. Estimating just the right spot, he pushed the button—and the car propelled forward. It felt as if the car had doubled its speed. Its booster rocket spewing flame from its rear exhaust, the Bugatti lifted off the ground and just managed to vault the barricades and congregated police vehicles, its tires scraping the cars' roofs, landing heavily on the other side amidst a showering of sparks and burning rubber. The trailing police vehicles slammed on their brakes, barely avoiding colliding into their parked colleagues.

The Wraith allowed himself the luxury of a small smile and pressed on, aiming to vanish before his hunters could fathom what had just taken place. Hitting top speed in an amazing fifty-five seconds, he knew he'd soon disappear from their view.

* * * * * *

Leena slipped quietly into the parked Cadillac—in use as a temporary replacement for the wrecked Daimler—startling Max almost as much as when The Wraith would appear from nowhere.

"How did it go?" he asked once composed.

"Fine," Leena replied, ripping off her mask. "Paul was right: there were more ninjas out there, though ninjas in name only."

"In name only?"

"They were dressed as ninjas, but hardly acted like them. They were shooting up everything in sight on Macquarie Street. I can only assume they were intended as a much more overt diversion than the Zombie Powder."

A weak sunshine was beginning to break, sending slivers of light sifting through the canyons of the city like the pinpoint beams of a laser. As Max started the car, Leena wondered as to Paul's progress and worried for his safety, and that of the country. Max guided the car out and into the morning traffic.

~ Chapter 14 ~

Still bustling about inside the large tent-like structure, Natalya Blackova's men moved hurriedly, preparing and installing various pieces of electronic equipment. Blackova stood regally to one side, watching the proceedings with an eager eye.

"Finish this quickly," she ordered. "The time of vengeance is near."

Khan entered, walking with a confident stride. He came up beside her. "Mistress, your plan is proceeding with perfection," he said. "Reports from Metro City have The Wraith being kept busy by our men. He has no knowledge of our presence here in Philadelphia nor of our plans to destroy the World's Fair and the US president."

Blackova slapped him with the back of her hand. "*My* men! *My* plans!"

"Yes, my mistress," Khan said, chagrined in tone but not batting an eyelash. He took a step back, allowing Blackova to step past him. "Everything has been installed within the grounds of the fair. We just have to complete the installation here."

"It is nearly time," Blackova said. "Ready the final preparations. I wish my statement to the world to be a grand one, and my men to be ready for a smooth transition of power...to me." She smiled seductively. She continued past Khan, and exited with a sashay of her hips.

* * * * * *

The storm had cleared. The sun beat down. The Wraith found himself in strange surroundings—and in action in broad daylight, something reserved only for the worst of emergencies. Patrolling the rooftops of a city now almost foreign to him, the Dread Avenger nevertheless had to make quick time to reach his destination: the Ritz-Carlton Hotel. He could see the hotel clear across town from his vantage point. He had ditched the car as soon as he had entered the city limits and moved to the upper reaches of the city, using his grapnel and line and jumping from building to building.

Springing into action, The Wraith sprinted over the rooftops as swiftly as possible. Time was of the essence, and he did not wish to linger long enough in the sunshine to be overly visible and arouse suspicion. When buildings were too far apart to be jumped, he used his grapnel and line to traverse the distances. Moving this way—avoiding the early morning hour traffic—proved most efficient. He soon found himself only a block or two from his target.

There, he said to himself. Across the street was Philadelphia's premier five-star luxury hotel, its neon beacon shining even in the brightness of the morning. The Wraith slowed, checked his watch. *Not much time left.* He had to make his move now, to give himself the maximum time to stop Blackova from causing her planned devastation. He ducked behind a chimney stack to avoid detection. On the hotel's roof across the way was a plethora of impeccably suited men—some of the president's Secret Service, keeping watch for potential assassins.

The Wraith sat, propped up against the chimney. *How do I handle this? Obviously, the Secret Service agents have to be taken care of to allow free passage to the president himself. But how?*

At that instant, a Secret Service agent appeared as if from nowhere. The Wraith had missed the agent when he first arrived on the scene. It made sense. Why wouldn't they have agents on the building across the street? The agent pointed his automatic at the scrunched down Dread Avenger.

"Stay right where you are!" the agent shouted.

The Wraith remained seated, but held his arms aloft in mock acquiescence. "You've captured me, Officer. Now take me to the president."

The agent ignored him and barked into the radio he had attached to his right shoulder. "I have a costumed perp cornered on the Meyer department store building roof. Require backup immediately."

Taking advantage of this ever-so-slight break in the agent's attention, The Wraith shot to his feet and wrenched the agent's gun from his hand. While holding the agent's wrist tightly in his right hand, The Wraith spun and lashed out with an elbow to the face, cracking the agent's dark sunglasses as well as his nose.

Reeling, the agent—as well trained as he no doubt was—had no chance. The Wraith executed a spinning scissor kick and connected with the Secret Service man's jaw, sending him crashing to the floor, comatose.

The Wraith spun on his heels. He had to act fast now that the entire available Secret Service had been alerted. He looked to the hotel's roof, and the urgency of the agents' movements there were clearly evident. He thought briefly to make a move directly for the president's window—for President Atworth was probably staying in the Presidential Suite—but almost instantly thought better of it. Secret Service personnel were well trained and expert marksmen. He would be shot down before he even reached the halfway point across the abyss separating the two buildings. *Quickly now, think.* He had it— knockout darts.

The Wraith removed from his belt what, to a stranger, would appear to be a small pan-pipe instrument. He manipulated the device so that, with a few turns of his hand, what emerged took on its true form: a blowpipe. From his current position, using it was impossible. He pulled his grapnel from his belt, and without further thought, fired it at the hotel, the grappling hook embedding deep into the concrete wall at the top near the hotel's ledge.

Roughly forty stories from street level, the Dread Avenger launched across the chasm. This maneuver required pinpoint timing, not-to-mention accuracy. The Secret Service agents, four of them that The Wraith could spot, had all stopped in their tracks at the sight of him flying headlong through the air. About halfway across, The Wraith took one hand off his line, and swiftly put the blowpipe to his lips and blew, aiming at the Secret Service man nearest him. *A direct hit.* He repeated the move toward the next agent, with the same result. He'd hoped this would not only take half his opponents out of the equation, but shock the other half just long enough to allow him to land safely on the roof of the hotel.

The Wraith landed on a narrow lower ledge, and immediately clambered up the remaining length of his attached line up over the ledge onto the roof, executing a flawless forward roll, then scurried behind the large air conditioning vent nearby. *Safety.* There were still two more Secret Service men—tall, burly fellows—to be dealt with. The Wraith could hear their approaching footsteps. He didn't want to hurt them; they were, after all, merely doing their jobs.

How were they to know I was here to save the president and not harm him? he thought.

He knew they wouldn't expect an open attack from his current location. Quickly, he threw himself out, catching the two Secret Service agents in mid-stride by surprise. The Wraith kept low, keeping himself below the sights of their drawn guns. He knew he had to first disarm them. The two agents were running side by side. The Wraith came at them from underneath, grabbed their gun arms and twisted their weapons free.

The two agents re-established their footing. Despite being impeccably attired in suits and dark sunglasses, their impressive musculature was not hidden from view. In such close quarters, they were unable to produce any other weapon they likely held on their person, and so hand-to-hand combat became the order of the moment. The Wraith ducked a blow from one of the agents, this one somewhat striking with his bleach-blond buzz-cut hairstyle. The Wraith immediately lashed out with a powerful punch to the gut of the other—a brown-haired, ruddy faced man—incapacitating him for the moment.

The blond agent contorted his face in anger. The Wraith smiled inwardly, knowing that this would make the agent sloppy, careless.

The agent reached under his coat, pulled another gun from a hidden holster, only to have the Dread Avenger kick the gun from his hand seconds later. The agent, furious, went on the attack, letting fly with kicks and punches that, had they connected, would have laid the Dread Avenger flat. The Wraith ducked and swerved as best he could, blocking blows with his forearm guards.

The agent appeared to be tiring, and The Wraith knew that time was running out fast. Noticing the other agent finally regaining his composure in the background, The Wraith rocked the blond-haired agent with a kick to the face, followed by a spinning kick to the head. The agent spun through the air, hitting the floor hard, unconscious.

The Wraith caught sight of the other agent from the corner of his eye, saw that he too was pulling another weapon from under his coat. Too far away to disarm him, The Wraith wrapped his cloak around his body, enveloping himself from head to shin in a protective barrier. The agent fired repeatedly, overzealously perhaps, but no doubt thinking it the only option with the president on site and in potential danger. The bullets bounced off The Wraith's cloak.

"What the hell?" the agent said, shocked.

Before the agent could react further, The Wraith emerged from his cloaked cocoon, grabbed the agent by the hand holding the gun, twisted that arm behind the agent's back aggressively and held him firmly.

"Call your colleagues. Tell them the situation has been contained. Assure them the president is safe," The Wraith growled in the hapless agent's ear.

"I won't..." the agent gasped. He winced in pain.

The Wraith applied more pressure to the agent's arm, pulling it to such an extent he thought it might soon snap if the agent wouldn't prove co-operative. "You will!"

The agent yelped. "All right...all right..." The guard angled his head toward his shoulder-radio. With his free hand, he flicked a switch. "Situation contained. I repeat, situation contained."

"Roger," came the reply over the radio. "The president is secure and will remain until the allotted hour."

"Roger," the agent replied.

The Wraith knew he had to take action instantly, for the agent was unlikely to comply so easily, especially not while in contact with his superiors. He thought it likely the agent would now attempt to alert the Secret Service, and considered it best to take the agent completely out of the equation. He smashed his elbow into the agent's head, sending him to sleep.

The Wraith's mind was whirling—he had to move fast; more agents were surely only seconds away. He had to reach the president. He spotted his line lying on the roof. He rushed over to the ledge, peered over and identified the largest window to the Presidential Suite. Grabbing a handful of line at a spot he estimated would enable him to reach the below window, he positioned himself carefully on the raised ledge—and dived. As the line snapped taut, he was propelled toward the large, ornate double windows. He let go of the line and crashed through the glass, landing heavily but securely on the floor of the suite amidst the raining debris of glass and timber.

"What the hell?" shouted a Secret Service agent, disbelief written all over his face.

The Wraith looked up to see a morass of armed agents surrounding President Atworth. No doubt they had been protecting him in readiness to secure his safe flight from the hotel. Guns were cocked and pointed in the Dread Avenger's direction.

"You just bought yourself some serious trouble, Mister," the agent at the lead of the procession said.

The Wraith raised his hands. There was no more need for violence. It was time for words. "Lower your weapons. I come on a mission of peace."

The lead agent took a few steps forward, smirking. "You can't be serious? You can't expect me to take the word of a costumed lunatic."

"Wait," an assured voice rang out from behind the throng of agents. "I want to hear what he has to say." President Atworth appeared—a fine, stern but honest looking gentleman with a charming mop of silver-grey hair on his head.

"Mr. President, I'd advise against that," the lead agent said. "This man works outside the law; he's a vigilante, The—"

"Wraith, I know," the president replied. "I've been following the news reports of his activities with great interest for a long time now. Let me through." The president moved forward to face The Wraith. The Dread Avenger kept his hands up in a gesture of peace.

President Atworth sidled up alongside him, with the Secret Service agents keeping aim on The Wraith.

"I met one of your kind when I was a kid. The Owl. Do you remember him? Ever since then..." The president stopped himself, perhaps afraid to reveal any semblance of hero-worship, but it was perhaps a little too late for that.

"I remember the Owl. He worked for the good of mankind. As do I," The Wraith said in a gentle tone. "Mr. President, please, I am not here to harm you, but to warn you."

"Warn me? Warn me about what?"

"There is a plan to assassinate you at the World's Fair this morning; to destroy the entire fair, in fact. You must stay away from the fair, I implore you." He made a conscious effort to be urgent in his tone.

The president paced the length of the suite, deep in thought.

"You cannot buy into any of this, Mr. President," the lead agent said angrily. "This man is a criminal. For all we know, he was sent here to assassinate you himself!"

President Atworth looked thoughtfully at the agent. "I hear you; I acknowledge what you're telling me." He turned to The Wraith. "And yet...my gut instinct tells me to believe this man." He smiled. "This may sound silly, but I've admired men like you since my childhood."

"But Mr. President—" the lead agent said.

"Oh, I know he operates outside the law, I know that full well," Atworth said. "And I don't condone such actions. Officially, I can't. But look at the good he has achieved in Metro City, where all others have failed." He paused, rubbing his chin, pensive. "I *do* believe him though." He faced the Dread Avenger. "Tell me everything you know."

~ Chapter 15 ~

The site of the Philadelphia World's Fair was packed full of carnival rides of every size and description, not to mention pavilions filled with exhibitions ranging from fine art to information promoting a variety of American cities, to farmers from across the country showing the finest samples of their produce and livestock. Staff members and exhibitors were bustling to and fro, going about their business, readying for the official opening in a couple of hours. The public wouldn't be allowed to enter until the official ceremony was completed and the president safely escorted away.

Huddled within the confines of one of the exhibitor tents, Natalya Blackova sat on her throne, constructed of the finest timber, the plush cloth backing of the seat and the regal bearing of the piece, made for a fine piece of furniture.

"It is time, Mistress," said Magnus Khan, standing in the open doorway. "The president will soon be arriving, and we must ready our escape from what will soon become a charred stain on the ground."

Blackova stood, her gown flowing elegantly over her hips and long legs. "Is everything in place? The remote workings in order? The men already off-site?"

"Yes, Mistress," Khan replied.

"Good," she said, ambling toward him. "As soon as the president arrives, we will make good our escape. And then, once we are a safe distance away, victory will be mine."

Blackova sauntered past him into the small antechamber section of the tent, ready to ensure the president had arrived before she left. She stood at the tent's front entrance, which offered an excellent view of the drive leading into the fair grounds. She smiled lasciviously when she soon spotted the president's limousine slowly making its way up the drive, escorted by a multitude of Secret Service men in cars, motor bikes and others on foot, running alongside the presidential motorcade.

"The president has arrived. We shall allow him to exit his car and move into position before making our own escape. There is plenty of time for us to flee and to create our intended havoc," Blackova said. She shut the door and turned to face Khan, who was still standing behind her. They strode back inside their tent.

"Transportation is ready for our escape," he said.

"There will be no escape for you!" a commanding voice rang out. The two whirled around to see The Wraith standing in the doorway.

* * * * * *

The Dread Avenger of the Underworld stood in the open doorway of the huge exhibitor's tent, his facial muscles tensed with fury, his hands curling into fists. He was finally reunited with those responsible for the slaughter of thousands of innocent people. They would not escape him this time.

"How can this be?" Blackova shrieked in outrage. "You are still in Metro City. We checked."

The Wraith laughed mockingly. "I discovered your plans and made arrangements to deceive you while I raced here. The president is safe."

The Wraith opened the door, giving the two villains a view of the drive outside. The president's limousine had parked just outside Blackova's tent, with a series of armed Secret Service agents exiting it and amassing outside the tent. The president was nowhere in sight.

"This is not possible," Blackova said in frustration. "Everything was planned to perfection. Vengeance is mine!"

"*Was.* Now only judgment remains," The Wraith said, moving forward, the Eyes of Judgment starting to crackle with fierce, ominous energy. Blackova took a careful step backward, but Khan remained rooted to the spot, glaring at him.

"Khan!" Blackova shouted.

Khan produced a small remote control device from a pouch on his left hip. "It is too late, Avenger. If we cannot destroy the president, then we will merely settle for destruction. Period."

Before The Wraith could react, Khan pressed the button on the device. A mighty roar erupted as if emanating from the very earth itself, deafening in its power. The force of the blast caused what felt like an earthquake, and The Wraith found it impossible to hold his ground and toppled to the floor. As he fell, he managed to catch a glimpse of the other two, also now prone on the tent floor.

While the fair was not yet open to the public, it was nevertheless teeming with exhibitors, handlers and staff, and the Dread Avenger could hear the desperate screams and panic of those caught in the maelstrom. A creaking sound caused him to look upward, just in time to see the tent roof tumbling down, covering those inside in seconds.

"Dammit!" he said. He struggled to find the nearby door, but the more he struggled, the harder the going became. In the tangled mess of the collapsed tent, there was no sign of the two villains. Of course, being covered as he was, he didn't expect to see them, but his highly acute senses could detect no sound or movement from his adversaries. He had to move quickly. Pulling a small knife from his belt, he plunged the blade into the fabric of the tent, and cut himself from his prison.

The Wraith stood and was met by a sight that chilled his soul. At least half of the fair—its buildings and carnival rides —were toppled or in flames. The smell of pain and death hung in the air. It was a sense the Dread Avenger had experienced all too often in recent times, and he was tired of it. The fact that the public had been spared this fate was of little cheer to him. As he feared, there was no sign of Natalya Blackova or Magnus Khan.

"Where did they go?" he shouted to the recovering Secret Service agents above the din.

"I...I think they went that way," one agent replied, pointing in their direction. He doubled over in pain, visibly wounded in the leg, no doubt with shrapnel from the blast.

"Call the emergency services; we need paramedics down here now!" The Wraith ordered, and ran in the direction the agent had indicated.

The devastation of the Philadelphia World's Fair blackened his mood. *I came here to save people, to stop this madness. I've failed.* The fact he'd saved the president and countless thousands *more* people was little consolation to him as he ran past dreadful scenes of destruction and massacre. He was tempted to step in, help as many of the survivors as possible, but he had to find Blackova and Khan. He couldn't risk them escaping once more. The sound of approaching ambulances soon eased his mind enough for him to focus on his primary mission—hunting the two down.

The fair's intricate and extremely large rollercoaster and Ferris wheel loomed over the Dread Avenger undamaged, its shadow casting deep pockets of blackness on the ground pockmarked with streams of light from the weak morning sunshine and the flickering shadows of the nearby flames.

As The Wraith rounded a battered kiosk stand blemished by flying debris, Magnus Khan leaped out, screaming in anger, taking him by surprise.

"RARRGGHHH!"

He ploughed into the Dread Avenger, sending them both crashing into the dusty ground. They struggled there, madly grappling and wrestling.

"Your plans are ruined, your mad quest for power ended," The Wraith said, lashing out with a powerful right to Khan's jaw. "You have lost!"

"You may be right, but the war is not yet over. You surely know that better than anyone, Wraith. There will be battles to come."

For a long time, the two gladiators began circling one another, sizing each other up. Khan reacted first, stepping forward, executing martial arts maneuvers of exceptional skill and technique. Kicks were ducked, sidestepped or blocked. Khan was putting up a ferocious fight. He no doubt knew this was the final battle, and the only option he had was to win it. Having battled Khan once before, The Wraith knew the villain's strengths and weaknesses, and knew he had to exploit them or all was lost. His plan was to avoid the battle as much as possible, keeping himself fresh and uninjured, while also tiring Khan out to such an extent as to make his defeat just that much easier. So far, it was working. He ducked, weaved and sidestepped as many of Khan's attempted blows as he could.

"You are weakening, Khan," The Wraith boomed. "You have nothing left."

"I have enough to take care of you, infidel," Khan said, breathing heavily.

Khan tried to re-assert control of the battle, tried to regain some sort of an advantage, swinging with blows that were now slower in speed and lacking in coordination. The Wraith was now able to execute his tactics to perfection. While Khan managed to connect with a blow or two, they were weak and ill-timed. Khan tried to execute spinning and scissor kicks, but they were slow and wobbly. The Wraith was able to dodge and weave the blows with more ease. Khan was visibly tiring; his breathing became more labored, his blows had little impact.

"I will not fall to the likes of you," Khan said in desperation.

Khan let fly with a right punch. The Wraith caught his fist. He gripped Khan's hand tightly—and squeezed. The Wraith reveled in the pain he was inflicting on Blackova's henchman. Khan tried to escape by throwing a weak left, but The Wraith caught it too—and squeezed again. Completely in the Dread Avenger's thrall, Khan submitted—unwillingly; struggling, but ultimately compliant—dropping to his knees in pain. The Eyes of Judgment energized to life.

"You whose evil knows no bounds," The Wraith said, "now is your time of just judgment."

Still squeezing with all the strength he could muster, The Wraith suddenly stopped, grabbed Khan by the wrappings around his throat, and pulled his head down and smashed his knee into Khan's face, shattering Khan's nasal septum.

"Feel the pain of each of your victims," The Wraith said. "Feel their shared pain a thousand-fold!"

The Wraith snatched Khan by his wrappings once more, jerked him up and pressed the villain's face toward the Eyes of Judgment. The Judgment Stare took hold of Khan, the electrical energy pulsing around Khan's face and head with a force and concentration The Wraith had never noticed before. Khan's eyes widened in shock, in sheer panic, as the pain and anguish of thousands shrouded him, invaded his soul—and Khan screamed. Blood curdling, terrifying.

The Wraith gripped him hard. Then he jerked Khan's face up, looking closely into it; even he was astounded by Khan's reaction. The sharpness of the light—the energy—emitted by the Eyes of Judgment caused The Wraith to squint, noticing the hair of Khan's Mongolian beard, his eyebrows, the hair on his head, melting away.

After a few more moments, The Wraith estimated Khan had had enough, and allowed the villain to drop into the dirt. Khan lay there, writhing as though having just experienced electric shock therapy, his hair singed, his face blank of expression, mumbling incoherently.

The Wraith took one look at the shell of the man at his feet, but betrayed no remorse, not for such a monster. His thoughts flashed back to Blackova. She had had plenty of time to, if not make her escape, at least hide within the fair's extensive grounds. He looked about, desperate to find her.

There, movement at the entry to the rollercoaster. Could that be her? It was hard to make out for sure at this distance, but it was in the path he estimated she would most likely have taken based on the direction that agent had pointed. He took a chance and went with his gut feeling. He sprinted in that direction. She wouldn't escape him. Not now.

* * * * * *

Leena paced the length and breadth of the Lair, frustrated at the lack of news from Paul.

Is he okay? Has he been able to save the president? Has Blackova and Khan been stopped? Captured? The questions tumbled around in her brain.

She wished Paul would contact her, tell her everything was okay, that his mission had been successful. Without any answers to soothe her irritation, she continued pacing, waiting.

"Leena," Max cried, suddenly appearing on the platform above. "I have news."

Max rushed down as fast as he could. Leena met him at the bottom of the elevator shaft.

"What? Tell me?"

"The radio just issued a bulletin. An explosion has ripped through the World's Fair. No reports of casualties yet, but they did say the event was clear of members of the public; apparently it hadn't yet been opened for them. The president's okay." Max said.

"And Paul?" Leena asked.

"No mention of the Chief. I'm sorry, Leena," he replied, "nor any mention of those responsible. The media seems to think it's the work of terrorists, which is their stock answer for everything these days, I guess."

She knew there would have been some fatalities at the fair, which saddened her, and she also knew the extra burden of guilt this would place on Paul's shoulders. The wait to hear more was killing her, but she also knew deep down that only one man could succeed against such incredible odds. She had to keep faith in that. She smiled wanly at Max, thanked him for the news, and continued her pacing.

* * * * * *

Racing as fast as he could, The Wraith soon reached the ticket stall to the giant rollercoaster. Blackova had already slipped through the gates and vanished from sight. The rollercoaster was surrounded by a high security fence, so it was likely that once inside, she was still there somewhere, hiding, and possibly waiting to pounce.

The Wraith squeezed through the jammed-shut ticket stall gates. This section of the fair was undamaged, though the carnage of what was destroyed was only a few hundred feet away. The Wraith slinked along slowly, watchfully. He attuned his razor-sharp senses for any sign of Blackova. There were none. He craned his head, but there was no sight of the evil temptress. He decided to sweep the perimeter of the area. Surely there would be some sign, some clue to her whereabouts.

As he made his way along the outer fence, in an anxious search for clues, the stark noise of the rollercoaster starting up diverted his attention.

Damn, he thought, *she's managed to secrete herself in the rollercoaster mechanism itself, turning it on.*

He backtracked at speed, just in time to catch sight of Blackova riding in a rollercoaster car—the first in a chain of eight cars linked together—slowly heading up the first steep incline. As her car rose, he reached the entryway to the ride and found no more cars on the tracks. Without further thought, he leapt up onto the tracks, and dashed along them.

Reaching the point where the track started its crescendo, The Wraith turned and looked upward. Blackova's car had already nearly reached the apex of the track. He considered what her next move might be.

She would have to leave the rollercoaster at some point. Riding the coaster in its entirety would only lead her back down...to me. That's not an option for her.

Then he saw Blackova's only means of escape. Right at the top of the ride, just before it twisted and turned in a complex series of loops, the rollercoaster jutted out close to the adjacent Ferris wheel.

Close enough to make a jump for it? That has to be it.

The Wraith wasted no more time. He pulled out his grapnel and fired it. The end of the line separated, becoming a miniature grappling hook, which plunked into the base of the track at the top of the coaster. He pressed the retract button on the grapnel, and was instantly and speedily hauled upward. In seconds, he was clambering up onto the track. The view from the top was staggering, as was the complete picture of the destruction wrought at Blackova's hands. At least three quarters of the expansive World's Fair site was in flames. Buildings had been reduced to rubble, lives completely destroyed.

Blackova will pay for this, he vowed, his wrath building.

The sight and sound of Blackova's car bearing down on him brought him back to the task at hand. With perfect timing, the Dread Avenger hurdled up and over the car, landing hard in the seat behind Blackova.

The Wraith rose, his cape flapping about him. "You're finished, Blackova. The reign of the Cobra dynasty has come to an end," he shouted over the ruckus of the high-speed car and the rustling wind.

"You haven't defeated me," Blackova shouted. "We will go on. Our dreams of conquest are never-ending, and despite this setback, we will return."

"We? There is no we, temptress. You are all alone. The Cobra is dead, the lackey Khan reduced to a babbling imbecile. And now there is only you."

Blackova looked at him with daggers in her eyes. Never before had The Wraith seen such a look in a woman's face; her hatred for him was palpable. She screamed and lunged at him, her icy fingers clutching at his throat. "Then I will take you with me. Let us embrace death together."

They struggled there, Blackova grappling with him, attempting to gouge his eyes. Her nails were long and as strong as steel. She carved a deep gash in his cheek, drawing blood. She reached for his throat. Despite her slight size and alluring shape, her hands were surprisingly strong, and The Wraith had trouble breaking her grip.

"A fitting end, is this not, for the man who destroyed everything I held dear?" Blackova spat in rage.

The Wraith answered with a vicious punch to the side of her head, finally causing her to release her grip. Despite the high, protective neckline of his costume, he was forced to hack the air back into his lungs. He couldn't imagine how strong she must be to be able to choke him through the ridgedness of his collar. Blackova leaned against the back of the front seat, hissed at him, then jumped to her left, soaring into empty space. At first stunned, The Wraith soon realized where they now were.

Of course—the Ferris wheel!

The Wraith flipped himself backward, up and over the rear of the car. He had to escape before the car entered into the loops and turns. It was the only way to ensure Blackova's capture. He jumped and landed hard on the tracks and rolled from the momentum, somehow twisting his knee in the process. He cried out from the pain.

He lay there for a few seconds, taking as long as he dared to catch his breath. He licked his lips; the coppery taste of his blood laced his tongue. Now, he reared up and saw Blackova barely hanging on to the outer railing of the immobile Ferris wheel, struggling to maintain her hold. Her jump had obviously been ill-timed, or perhaps she had been weakened or tired by her battle with him.

The Dread Avenger stood and limped over to the edge of the track, getting as close as possible to the imperiled Blackova.

"You were right, Wraith," Blackova called out. "This *is* the end."

"Try and gain a foothold. You can't hang there forever," he said.

Her fingers slipping, her grip failing, Blackova said nothing, but smiled weakly at the Dread Avenger—and let go. She made no sound as she fell to her death, the dusty ground of the fairground expanse a fitting resting place for such as her. And yet, through her demise, The Wraith felt no peace, no satisfaction. Only the heavy weight of so many lives, lost needlessly, pressing down upon him like a lead weight. Their deaths twisted his soul. Leena often chided him on taking too much burden upon himself, but along with his many gifts, there was also this curse, and as with many things both good and bad, they always came hand-in-hand.

~ Chapter 16 ~

Paul rested comfortably in his bed, his right knee tightly bandaged, his left cheek patched up. His body was mending fast and sure; his powers increased his body's natural healing abilities five-fold, but it was not the condition of his body that worried Leena so, but his mind. Leena sat at the edge of the bed and watched his blank expression with concern.

"I've never seen the Eyes of Judgment have such an affect on anyone before," Paul said, his gaze downcast.

"Do you have any idea why?"

"I can't be sure, but...perhaps because this was the first time the Judgment Stare has judged someone as evil as Khan. He was responsible, personally and by collusion, for the wanton slaughter of thousands of people. Maybe that caused the Eyes to go into overdrive, to truly punish Khan for his malevolence." Paul looked down into his lap and, for a few moments, silence reigned.

"We've found a place for Adam," Leena finally said, trying to lighten Paul's dark mood. "He's no longer determined to live the life of a hermit. His training will start soon." Paul showed no emotion to this. "Darling, you've got to pull yourself out of this."

"Leena...so many lives were lost, so many people died because I failed to stop Blackova in time," he said. "That's not something I can easily forget."

She sighed and edged closer by his side. "You cannot be responsible for the entire world, no matter how hard you try. You're only one man; there is only so much you can do. You *did* stop her. You saved the president and countless more lives. Isn't that enough?"

Paul looked up at her with forlorn eyes. "It's not enough. It's never enough."

She leaned down and kissed him, then they embraced. Where all else failed, love conquered all.

* * * * * *

The feeble cries of the insane rang out through the corridors of the Metro City Asylum for the Criminally Insane. It was a large building, a remnant of better times, and, as with many public buildings within the city, it had now fallen on harder times. Its walls boasted crumbling paintwork and masonry, its windows were grubby, the curtains were tattered. It was within these walls that Magnus Khan found himself, safely secured in a padded cell, restricted in movement by a tightly-fitted straight jacket. He sat there, immobile, his features changed somewhat by his recent experience. His hair was still singed, his eyes almost completely opaque.

"He is coming, he is coming, he is coming..." he repeated over and over.

The meaning of his words, if there were any to be had, would not be revealed by him right now. No doubt only time would tell...

~ Author's Note ~

It's been a long time since I've really looked at this book, and I'm happy to say it's held up very well since I conceived and wrote it eight years ago. I'm very proud of it, written as it was during a difficult part of my life. I hope you all enjoyed it.

As always, I need to thank a few people, which I will proceed to do now. To my wife goes the greatest thanks. Jennifer is always there for me, loving and caring for me, and her literary advice is always welcome. To my family, thank you for always being there for me also. To my Trinity Comics team—Jeff Welborn, Roland Bird, Joel Danford, Jeff Austin, Adam O. Pruett, Rick Hannah and Splash!, thanks for always making me look better than I actually am. I must also thank the great (now sadly deceased) Al Rio for supplying such a wonderful cover, which was also used as the cover for the original hardcover release in 2006. Thanks also go to D.P. Lyle M.D. for his excellent book *Murder and Mayhem*, which provided exceptional research material for this novel (eg. the Zombie Powder); and to Norvell Page, whose brilliant and groundbreaking work on *The Spider* pulp magazine (among others) back in the 1940s inspired me to create The Wraith in the first place. Those stories still thrill and entertain all who read them to this day, nearly seven decades later. I can only hope my stories have a fraction of that longevity.

Following this is a sneak peek at the next book in *The Wraith Adventures* series, *Cult of the Damned*. Details on how to purchase this book are also contained in the following pages.

Thank you.

Frank Dirscherl
Wollongong NSW, 2013

CULT OF THE DAMNED
~ Sneak peek ~

Here is a special sneak peek at the following novel in the series, *Cult of the Damned*. Please enjoy chapter 1 of this exciting book...

~ Prologue ~

The rain pummeled down from the night sky in sheets as thick as lead. The furious onslaught from the heavens lashed the windshield of the armored truck as it rumbled down the busy Metro City thoroughfare. Life never took a breather in a city like Metro, and even at 4 A.M. in such inclement weather, the streets were teeming with people and cars of all descriptions. Car horns blared, certain people—johns, hookers, bums, cops—mill about, yelling, weeping, running, fighting. Night was always a bleak time in Metro City, and this night was no exception.

"Man, what a time to be delivering this cargo," Ralph said from the passenger seat of the armored truck. "Why the heck do we get stuck with all the crap jobs, Jim?" Ralph was a burly, heavy-set man in his fifties with a full, graying mustache and heavily-lidded eyes. He shifted uncomfortably in his seat, while his partner peered intently through the windshield, trying to keep control of the truck in the appalling conditions.

Jim shrugged his shoulders. "And why do we have to deliver this thing at this ungodly hour?"

"Because Mr. Latham told us to," said Ralph, who noted Jim's sour expression. He sighed. "Mr. Latham thought it best to deliver such valuable cargo at a time when there was the least chance of anything going wrong. That work better for you?"

Jim, younger, slimmer and less hairy than his co-pilot, arched an eyebrow. "Yeah, but that doesn't reflect well on us though, does it? I can't wait to get rid of it. Darn thing gives me the creeps."

"Ah well. Latham pays for the service, so who are we to argue?"

"What is it exactly anyway?" Jim queried. "Some voodoo piece?"

"I don't know, and I don't really care. All I know is we were warned it shouldn't be touched under any circumstances. Something about it being dangerous. Beats me how, though."

Jim shivered at the mention of the word *dangerous*.

The truck inched its way through the torrential rain, down the hectic Montgomery Street, swarming as it was with that particular brand of nightlife for which Metro had long since become infamous. Red light turning green, Jim veered into the narrower Harris Street, and then out into the wider expanse of Joseph Boulevard.

"Are you sure we're going the right way?" Jim asked, guiding the truck as best he could down the wide, lengthy road. He fiddled with the de-frost controls on the truck's dashboard, trying to get it working but without much luck. The windshield was fogged over.

"Yeah, yeah, turn here," Ralph replied. He removed a handkerchief from his right-side trouser pocket, and wiped the windshield clear as best he could.

Jim moved the truck onto George Avenue and finally toward the looming Metro City Gallery. The lights of the gallery shone through the foggy windshield in bright blotches as the truck turned and drove carefully up the short drive, coming to a halt at a security gate.

Jim wound down his window. "Hey, where do we deliver this?" he asked the guard in the small booth beside them.

"You the special delivery guys?" the guard shouted above the din of the pouring rain. Jim nodded. "Go round the turn there and then head to the back." The guard thumbed to somewhere further down the drive.

"Yeah, okay. Sure thing," Jim said and rolled up the window. "I'll be glad to hand this stuff over and get back home. I can just catch a few hours sleep before my next shift. I hate night shifts." He drove the truck further down the drive as directed.

"Especially in this kind of weather," Ralph said. "You think it's ever going to stop raining? How long's it been, two weeks? I'm practically growing gills already."

"I read in the paper it's expected to rain most of this month. Climate change they call it," Jim said, as he parked the truck in the circular loading zone protected from the elements by a large overhead awning. "C'mon, let's get this over with."

The two security officers exited the truck and moved back to the vehicle's rear door, the sound of their footsteps barely distinguishable from that of the rain. They looked up to see a tall, well-dressed man with thinning hair and a grin that would make the Cheshire Cat green with envy approaching them from the gallery's loading dock. He was flanked by several uniformed armed guards, ready to take possession of the truck's goods.

"Gentlemen, my name is Bartholomew Gregory. I'm the curator of this gallery," greeted the curator in a hearty tone. "I am so glad to see you've arrived with our invaluable artifact."

"What is this we're hauling, exactly? Some voodoo stone or something?" Jim asked while opening the truck's rear door.

"An artefact that is absolutely priceless," Gregory said, still smiling. "The Cortes Stone, an ancient Aztec stone carving, depicting one of their gods, Huitzilopochtli, defeating the invading Spaniards led by Hernando Cortes. It was only recently discovered in the wilds of Mexico in a heretofore undiscovered tomb. Our great patron, Robert Latham ensured this international treasure would make its home here as part of this city's two-hundredth anniversary celebration."

Ralph looked to Jim and rolled his eyes. Jim knew what he meant. *Is this guy reading off a cue card?*

"Well, here's your precious carving, packed away nice and tight," Ralph said, indicating inside the truck.

"I cannot thank you enough for your vigilance and speedy arrival here. I shall make sure Mr. Latham hears of your exemplary work," Gregory said. The curator indicated his own guards to take charge of the situation, which they promptly did, surrounding the truck carefully, their guns raised in readiness for any eventuality. From the rear of the loading dock several workmen appeared, dressed in overalls, one of whom pulled a metallic trolley behind him.

"Uh, yeah, well, thanks," Ralph said, scratching his head with the one hand while brandishing a clipboard with the other. "Now, if you could just sign here, Mr.—"

"Over there, please be careful with the package," Gregory shouted to one of the workmen, ignoring Ralph. "It's your jobs if you drop it."

Two of the workmen climbed into the truck and removed the fastenings securing the wooden crate to the truck floor.

They then carefully shifted the large crate to the edge of the truck, then onto the awaiting trolley.

"Now, let's get this inside and away from this atrocious weather," Gregory said, turning on his heels and quickly making his way back into the gallery. The workmen, with the secured carving, followed suit, the gallery's security guards remaining on alert.

"Uh...Mr. Gregory?" Ralph shouted, waving his clipboard. "Could you—" But Gregory had already disappeared, vanishing within the bowels of the city gallery. Ralph looked to Jim, who merely shrugged his shoulders. "C'mon, we have to get this guy's signature before we can leave."

They strode the path down into the loading dock and climbed the stairs up into the main loading area. They were greeted by a plethora of crates and boxes of all sizes and lighting so low as to be almost sinister, the boxes and crates casting eerie shadows on the walls surrounding them.

"Where'd they get to?" Jim asked, stumbling around in the darkness.

"Over there." Ralph pointed. "There's some light."

The two arrived at a partially-open wooden door. A weak light shone from the other side. Peering round, Jim saw a long, narrow corridor snaking down toward a murky center.

"Take a look," Jim said and let Ralph grab a peek.

"I guess they went that way," Ralph said, again scratching his head.

They passed through the corridor, entered the larger, darkened room beyond, then heard voices coming from yet another room, the entrance to which lay ahead of them.

"This way. Let's just get this signed so we can get outta this maze," Ralph muttered.

They passed through this last doorway to find themselves in a large, cavernous area with high glass ceilings and low, moody lighting. The rain beat down on the glass, its steady drum rumbling throughout the room. Paintings and etchings of incredible beauty and intricacy lined the walls. Bartholomew Gregory and three of his workmen stood at the far side of the room. The armed guards were nowhere in sight.

"Careful. The stone is the most precious piece we've ever received," Gregory said.

As the two security officers walked over to join him, two of the three workmen cautiously pried open the wooden crate containing the carving.

"Mr. Gregory, we need your—" Ralph started to say but was cut off by a wave of the hand.

"Hmm...? Oh, yes, one moment please," the curator replied absently.

With the wooden crate open, a gloved workman lifted a small, rounded, stone slab roughly twelve inches in diameter above the rim of the crate. Gregory's eyes shone bright at the sight of it. The surface of the stone was decorated with carvings of unique and complex beauty, with depictions of various figures that neither Jim nor Ralph recognized.

"It's even more beautiful than I could have ever imagined," Gregory said under his breath. "See the great sun god wreaking vengeance on the Conquistadors? And here," he indicated to one of the figures on the carving, "on Cortes himself. A depiction of the Aztec Indians greatest desire, and one which they sadly never realized." He stopped to catch his breath. "And the jade embossing the rim...it is an amazing piece." Gregory straightened. "Put it over there." And nodded toward the stand, shaped much like a speaker's lectern, nearby.

The workman holding the stone laid it gently into its ready-made cradle at the top of the stand.

"Good," Gregory said, still marveling over the stone. "I find I cannot take my eyes off this. It's as though I..."

He moved closer to the object. "I need to—" He reached out to touch the carving, to run his fingers along its elaborate imagery of godly vengeance.

"Mr. Gregory, no!" Ralph cried.

But it was too late.

Gregory's face lit up in apparent ecstasy as he felt the texture of the stone and its carvings, then lurched backward, coughing, his body heaving violently. He collapsed in a heap on the gallery floor—and quickly disintegrated into ash before the shocked eyes of those present.

~ Also Available ~

The Wraith Adventures #1

THE WRAITH

Frank Dirscherl

In a world not far removed from our own, a city lies ravaged.
Crime overruns its streets; its citizens are helpless. Crime lord
Robert Latham, to the world at large a legitimate businessman,
holds the city in his sway. Fear and intimidation rule throughout.
One man stands above the rest, willing to fight for freedom.
That man is The Wraith.
ISBN: 978-0-646-90689-8

NOW AVAILABLE!

www.trinitycomics.com

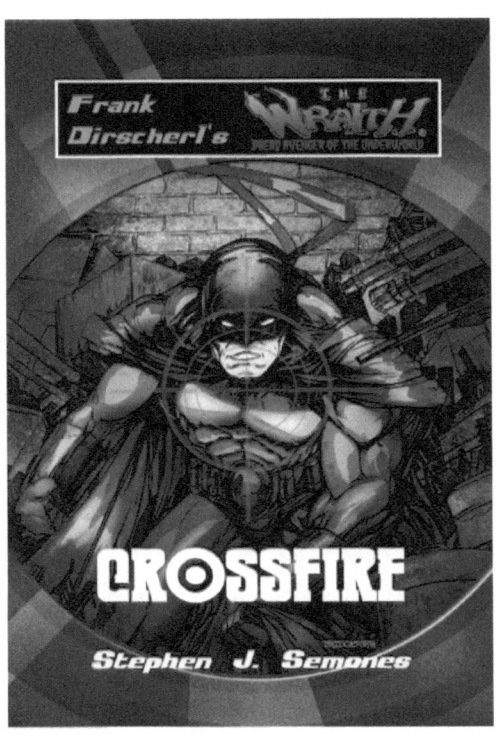

The Wraith Adventures #2.5
CROSSFIRE
Stephen J. Semones; edited by Frank Dirscherl

After a terrorist attack leaves the citizens of Metro City reeling, an enigmatic stranger emerges from the wake of the destruction to wage war on local crime-lord Robert Latham. In the midst of this, Max Horton, The Wraith's right-hand man, vanishes without a trace. Searching for Max, and for those responsible for the devastation, The Wraith sets out for answers.
ISBN: 978-0-646-58377-8

NOW AVAILABLE!

www.trinitycomics.com

The Wraith Adventures #3
CULT OF THE DAMNED
Frank Dirscherl

With the city back firmly in his grasp, crime lord and
entrepreneur Robert Latham is celebrating by bankrolling Metro
City's 200th anniversary gala year, which includes the unveiling of a
never-before-seen ancient Aztec stone carving—the Cortes Stone—at
the City Gallery, a carving that has thrilled the scientific and
artistic communities, but infuriated the monstrous Aztekoth.

NEW EDITION AVAILABLE SOON!

www.trinitycomics.com

The Wraith Adventures #4

CRY OF THE WEREWOLF

Frank Dirscherl

Having gone through ordeal after ordeal, Paul Sanderson (aka The Wraith Dread Avenger of the Underworld ®) and his love Leena Patterson, decide to take a long overdue vacation. However, their idyll is soon shattered by an attack by a creature nobody thought could possibly exist—a werewolf. Soon, an evil so heinous makes himself known, and only The Wraith could possibly defeat it.
ISBN: 978-0-646-57757-9

AVAILABLE NOW!

www.trinitycomics.com

The Wraith comic book series

THE WRAITH: THE COLLECTED EDITIONS #1-3

Frank Dirscherl and a variety of artists

The adventures of the Dread Avenger of the Underworld in comic
book format. The trade paperback collecting issues #1-3 of the
series. Including each issue's color cover. Over 100 pages of action
and excitement.
ISBN: 978-1-4710-4977-4

AVAILABLE NOW!

www.trinitycomics.com

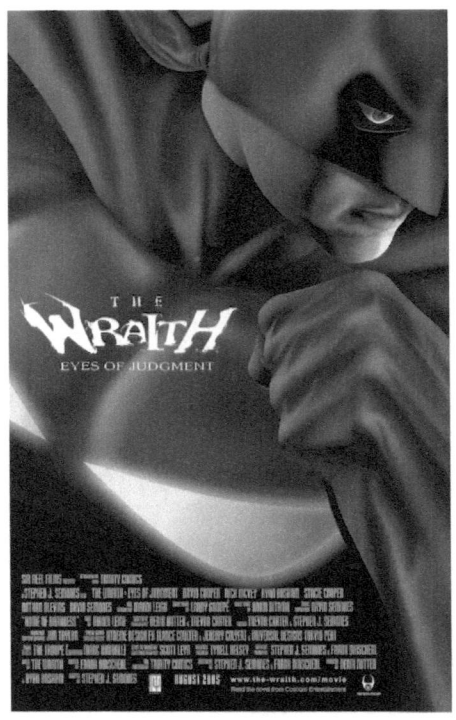

The Wraith short film on DVD
THE WRAITH: EYES OF JUDGMENT

This Special Edition 2-disc DVD, based on the novel *The Wraith*,
features over four hours of special features spanning two
impressive discs. With animated menus mixed in digital surround
sound, this will satisfy even the most hardcore DVD enthusiasts.
ASIN: B000F3ZTFS

AVAILABLE NOW!

www.trinitycomics.com

Want to be The Wraith?

Well, it might be hard to actually *be* The Wraith, unless of course you, too, have been endowed with the power of the Eyes of Judgment. But you can certainly dress, drink and drive like him [*] (and you don't always have to be a millionaire to do so). See for yourselves.

The Wraith/Paul Sanderson wears:

- bespoke clothing from Shanghai C&G Fashion Ltd. – www.bespokesuit.en.ec21.com
- bespoke shoes from Shanghai Tianzi Shoes – www.aliexpress.com/fm-store/702551
- watches from Christopher Ward www.christopherward.co.uk

drinks:

- Twinings Earl & Lady Grey tea – www.twinings.co.uk
- The Balvenie Scotch whisky – www.thebalvenie.com
- Armand de Brignac champagne – www.armanddebrignac.com

---

[*] Please note: Trinity Comics does not condone drinking and driving. **All** adults, please always drink responsibly and never drink and drive

uses:

- Toshiba laptops - www.toshiba.com
- Chesterfield furniture from Abbey Furniture
  www.chesterfieldfurnituremelbourne.com.au

drives:

- a Bentley Continental GT - www.bentleymotors.com

And, if you're really eager to actually look like The Wraith—in full costume—then you can always head over to Xtreme Design FX and let Lance Coulter there make you an exact replica of the costume used for The Wraith motion picture - www.xtremedesignfx.com

www.ingramcontent.com/pod-product-compliance
Lightning Source LLC
Chambersburg PA
CBHW020953180626
46814CB00003B/1077